LAUNCHED

LAUNCHED

VICTOR RAPPOPORT

authorHOUSE®

AuthorHouse™
1663 Liberty Drive
Bloomington, IN 47403
www.authorhouse.com
Phone: 1-800-839-8640

Published by AuthorHouse   06/28/2013

ISBN: 978-1-4817-7289-1 (sc)
ISBN: 978-1-4817-7288-4 (e)

Library of Congress Control Number: 2013911764

CHAPTER 1

In the spring of 1999, Ivan Sakalov, accompanied by his wife Agasha and daughter Katya flew in a Cessna from Moscow to Grozny, Chechnya. Ivan couldn't stay with them in Grozny, since he had pressing business back in Moscow. But it would give him a chance to spend precious time with them on their flight.

A secret government project in Moscow demanded Ivan full time. He hadn't had a vacation in years. His daughter was growing up and he had missed birthdays and holidays. Agasha had wanted to go to Grozny since she was a little girl. Her parents were born in Grozny and she spent her childhood there. Unfortunately, her mother and father were killed in 1996 when Boris Yeltsin had his Russian forces attack the town. Both parents were burned to death in their house.

"Mommy look". Katya pointed to the landing strip as the airplane approached the Grozny airport. Her wispy blond hair was falling in her eyes. Agasha pushed her hand gently across Katya's forehead and pulled her daughter's hair back in a pony tail. She fished through her purse for a rubber band to secure it.

Ivan watched the mother daughter interaction. He was so glad he took the trip. His wife and daughter were his life.

"Daddy, we're here".

"Yes Katya, we're here". He bent over and kissed his daughter on the forehead. His wife reached over and squeezed his hand.

They shared a loving look and then prepared for landing. After the plane landed, Ivan helped Agasha and Katya with their luggage and flagged down a cab.

"You mind your mommy", he told his daughter, never doubting she wouldn't. She was like her mother, beautiful inside and out. Agasha was the love of his life. He felt such emptiness before he met her. And now he had a family. His life was full. He put them in the cab and kissed them goodbye while the driver loaded the luggage.

"You're sure you have enough money?"

"Ivan, we are only going for a week. You've given me enough money to live on for a month".

"Daddy said I can buy toys, mommy".

"Of course you can, darling. Whatever daddy says". She flashed a smile at Ivan. They had been married for ten years, and she could still melt his heart with that smile. Agasha had the cab driver take her and Katya to the hotel where they were staying. The driver helped them take their luggage into the hotel and Agasha paid him a little extra. The hotel clerk checked them in and they went up to their room. It was getting late so they went out to a restaurant right near the hotel and shared a fancy dinner. Then they went back to the hotel, got into bed and drifted off to sleep. The next day Agasha could hardly wait to get to the marketplace on the outskirts of Grozny where her parents used to take her when she was a child. It was a beautiful spring day and there were hundreds of shoppers purchasing items from vendors at outdoor stands. Agasha and Katya were picking out oranges at one of the stands.

"Your father likes seedless oranges" said Agasha to Katya.

"Ok, mommy", said Katya.

Suddenly, out of nowhere came two large military missiles which exploded right above the market place, leveling everything and killing everyone including Agasha and Katya.

Ivan had just sent his secretary out to get him lunch when he was called about the news of the missile strike and the deaths of his wife and daughter which totally devastated him. He dropped the telephone, passed out and fell to the floor. When he came to, he called one of his friends in the Russian underground who told him that Andre Zubov, a member of the State Duma and who had tremendous political clout in Russia and who hated the Chechnyns had convinced President Yeltsin that the particular marketplace where Agasha and Katya were killed was a front where Chechnyan separatists purchased weapons and that's why the President allowed Zubov to authorize the missile strike. Now, years later Ivan Sakalov was going to get his revenge.

Leontiev Mikhail, a slender gray haired man in his sixties was the engineer on a freight train leaving Minsk for Moscow. The thirty six box cars were carrying thousands of bags of cement except for one box car which was carrying large bags of cocaine worth many millions of rubles. Before leaving Minsk, Leontiev was told by his son Vladimir who was one of the leaders of the Solntsevos, a large Russian mafia group, that illegal cargo was going to be in one of the box cars, and that he was to stop the train when he saw a large black truck parked near the tracks. The money that the Solntsevos was going to get when the cocaine was sold was going to be sent to California to finance sixty phony medical clinics and dozens of mobile laboratories where patients would be promised free physical examinations and diagnostic tests. The Solntsevos members would then submit fraudulent bills, supported by falsified medical reports and treatment forms to insurance companies claiming the clinics provided medical services prescribed by doctors. These types of false claims could bring almost a billion dollars and the money would then be laundered through hundreds of shell companies and foreign banks.

Since the Solntsevos were responsible for getting him his job as a train engineer, Leontiev could not refuse their request. Therefore, halfway between Minsk and Moscow when Leontiev saw the large black truck parked beside the train tracks he stopped the train next to the truck. Eight men jumped out of the truck and removed the bags containing the cocaine from the train after which Leontiev continued on to Moscow. What Leontiev did not know was that one of the bags of cocaine broke inside the box car and when the train was cleaned in Moscow, the cleaning company called the police when they found cocaine all over the box car floor. Leontiev was arrested and tried by a judge with no jury. Leonitev remained silent during the entire trial and was found guilty of transporting cocaine into Moscow. At the end of the trial, Leontiev was sentenced to thirty years in prison. Leontiev knew if he were to betray the Solntsevos and tell the court who the real culprits were, he would be tortured and killed by the Solntsevos whether he was in prison or found not guilty and set free. Besides, Leontiev would never do anything that might bring the law down on his sons Vladimir and Yuri.

It was midnight inside Butyrskaya Prison in Moscow. Leontiev was sitting alone in his small prison cell, when two prison guards came in. A prisoner across the hall who was looking through the small window in his cell door, saw what was happening.

"Where is the cocaine, Leontiev?" asked one of the guards. Leontiev didn't say a word. "We asked you before and now we ask you for the last time". He remained silent the same way he did one month before during his trial. Leontiev didn't even acknowledge the guards' presence in his cell. Leontiev wouldn't speak so the guards climbed on top of Leontiev and choked him to death, then they left the cell. The next morning the prisoner who saw the killing was talking on a wall mounted telephone. A guard behind the wall, out of the prisoner's sight, was listening on another telephone. That night a dead body was found on the ground next to a fence inside the prison. It was the prisoner who was on the wall telephone that morning.

The next day, Warden Glasov was sitting in a chair behind his desk in his office. Vladimir Mikhail, big, gorilla like, short hair, clean shaven and his brother, Yuri Mikhail, small and thin, long hair and beard, were standing in front of Glasov's desk glaring at him.

"The inmates that belong to the Solntsevos mafia were the ones who killed your father" Glasov said to the Mikhail brothers. Vladimir knew the warden was lying because Vladimir was the person the prisoner on the wall telephone called the day before and told him he saw the guards kill his father. Vladimir stared at the warden and yelled.

"Don't lie to us Warden Glasov! We know who killed him. It was your men because they wanted our father to tell what happened to the cocaine that was supposed to have been on the train he was taking from Minsk to Moscow. Even if he knew where the cocaine was, he wouldn't have betrayed the Solntsevos or they would have killed him." Warden Glasov jumped up and pointed to the door.

"Get out". Vladimir and Yuri slowly walked out of the office backwards, staring at Warden Glasov. They knew that they could be in trouble themselves if they went forward with their accusation against the guards because there was no possible way to prove that the guards killed their father. But Vladimir had a plan that would punish the Russian government for what they did to his father. It was early evening the next day when Vladimir dialed Ivan's telephone number. Ivan was driving his car down a busy Moscow street. Sitting next to Ivan was his secretary Trishka Perova, a very pretty blond haired, blue eyed woman in her twenties. Ivan's cell phone rang. He opened it and listened to Vladimir talking to him. then he said into the phone.

"Thank you Vladimir I'll be forever grateful and I'll take care of it for you. I have everything I need with me".

Ivan clicked off his cell phone and Trishka gave him a nasty look when he made a quick U turn and drove back the way he came. Then he slowed down and parked the car in front of the large building where he and Trishka worked. Trishka asked impatiently.

"What are you doing Ivan?"

"I have to go back to the office and get some papers I forgot to take with me."

Trishka was upset and tired from losing so much sleep the night before after her boy friend of over one year told her yesterday that he was leaving her for another woman. Trishka was shocked at this revelation because they had just recently made plans to have a wedding in two months. She had even purchased a beautiful wedding dress that was hanging in her closet. If she knew Ivan wasn't going to take her directly home after work like he told her he would do while they were at the office, she would have had her friend Lena drive her home instead.

She gave him a nasty look as he got out of the car. He closed the door, opened the trunk and took out a large leather briefcase. Then he walked up to the building and used his electronic key to open the door. Ivan walked in and waved at the guard standing inside.

"I left some papers in my office, Belinski".

"Everyone else is gone mister Sakalov, so please take your time."

Ivan entered the elevator, and pushed the button. The door closed and the elevator began its ascent. Ivan got out at the fourth floor and walked down the hall to a double door, took a key ring out of his pocket and opened the doors with one of the keys. Then he went over to a monster computer that took up the entire side of the room. Ivan removed a small rectangular metal box from his briefcase and opened a door in front of the computer with one of his keys. Then he put the small box on a shelf behind the door he opened, and began typing on the keyboard. The little box suddenly began flashing red. There was a strange humming sound coming from the guts of the computer. Lights were flashing on the monitor. The humming suddenly stopped. Ivan put the tiny box that was still flashing red back into his briefcase. Then he took explosive devices out of his briefcase and shoved one against the computer and set the timer on the device. He walked around the office setting more explosives with timers in strategic places. Then he got in the elevator and pushed the fifth floor button. The elevator went up one floor and stopped. Ivan got out and set more explosive devices in areas on the fifth floor, next to a large gas container. He knew that the natural gas in the container was flowing through pipes to every room in the building for heating purposes and causing the gas container to explode could destroy the entire building. Guard Belinski was not at his station when the elevator door opened on the first floor and Ivan stepped out. Ivan was extremely upset that he could not find Belinski and take him out of the building because Ivan knew that Belinski would be killed when the building was destroyed, but it was too late to change the explosive timers which were set to go off in less than one minute. Ivan quickly pushed his electronic key through the front door exit lock. The door opened and Ivan ran to his car. As he and Trishka sped away from the building there was a giant explosion, then another. Later, Ivan and Trishka were in her apartment watching the news on television. The building where they worked which housed the giant computer was now a mountain of twisted steel and rubble. The television showed an emergency crew pushing a gurney with the body of Belinski toward an ambulance that was parked in the street next to the burned out building.

"I'm sorry about Belinski, Trishka. But I promised Vladimir Mikhail, the boss of the Solntsevos a Russian mafia group that I'd destroy the building if he would kill the man who caused the deaths of my wife and daughter in 1999, when the Russians fired missiles into Grozny's central market place where they were shopping. Andre Zubov, who's still a member of the State Duma was behind the missile attack. Zubov convinced President Yeltsin that the market place was used by Chechen separatists as a bazaar where they could purchase weapons." Trishka stared hysterically wide eyed at Ivan as he continued.

"Vladimir Mikhail wanted revenge against the Russian leaders who had his father killed in prison. Vladimir told me he would kill the son of a bitch Andre Zubov for me if I would get him the tiny building block materials inside the existing K Fifty Five computer then destroy the computer and all of the materials relating to the

K Fifty Five which were stored in the building. Then he could sell the secret materials I got for him to the Russians for more than three hundred million rubles. I did what he asked after he cut Zubov's head off this morning".

Trishka watched the television showing the medics putting Belinski's body into the ambulance. She remembered the good times she and Belinski had when he took her to the mountains on their vacation two years ago. They rented a small cabin. It was snowing and she and Belinski went skiing during the day. When night fell Trishka and Belinski stayed in the cabin where she cooked dinner. They didn't have sex but they danced to slow music that Belinski played on the record player that he brought to the cabin. All she could remember about Belinski were the happy times they spent together on that trip to the mountains. Trishka couldn't believe the terrible feelings she had inside of her towards Ivan as she turned to him and looked at him with total hatred in her eyes.

"Belinski was my friend and you killed him".

"Belinski wasn't at his station when I left the building. I couldn't find him in time. I'm so sorry Trishka". She yelled back at him.

"Sorry! . . . you Chechen bastard, get out of my apartment!"

Trishka walked toward the front door to open it. Ivan was right behind her. She didn't see him pick up the large bottle of wine from a table. Ivan slammed her in the head with it, knocking her out. Ivan knew he had to prevent Trishka from going to the police and he had an idea that he knew would change his life as well as hers forever.

CHAPTER 2

Trishka was unconscious, face down on an operating table in Doctor Afons Gorchakov's clinic. Her hands were tied behind her back and a piece of duct tape covered her mouth. Ivan had made an arrangement with the doctor to pay him well for what he was about to do to Trishka. Ivan knew the doctor would do as he was told, because he had just gone through a divorce and was almost bankrupt. Doctor Gorchakov promised Ivan that everything he did that day to Trishka would remain a secret. Ivan told Gorchakov to leave the room, after which Ivan carefully removed a microchip from inside the flashing red box with tweezers. The fragment was also flashing red. Ivan put the microchip inside a tiny round piece of lead, then sealed the opening in the piece of lead with a soldering iron that was on a table in a tray. Ivan went into the hall and motioned for Doctor Gorchakov to come back into the room and told him to inject the microchip into Trishka's head. The doctor put the tiny round bead in a syringe with liquid, then shoved the needle into the base of Trishka's skull. He let the liquid with the bead flow into her. Trishka's body convulsed. He pulled the needle out and put the syringe down.

"Now, the money" said doctor Gorvhakov, holding out his hand. Ivan handed the doctor a roll of bills. The doctor counted it.

"I want more than this because it was more difficult than I thought it would be".

"That was our deal" said Ivan. The doctor held out his hand again.

"If you don't give me more money, I'll make your life a living hell". Ivan raised the soldering iron and doctor Gorvhakov screamed when Ivan stabbed him in the head with it. Ivan was in his car driving across town and Trishka was asleep in the back seat. The tiny flashing red box was on the front seat next to Ivan. He patted the box, then whispered to it.

"Even if I lose you I still have your information because every bit of it is inside her head." He laughed as he put the flashing box in his pocket.

Ivan stopped the car in Trishka's underground parking space then carried her out of the car up to her apartment. He took the keys from her purse, opened the door to the apartment and put her on the living room couch. Trishka was very groggy as she rubbed the back of her head and looked up at Ivan who was standing next to the couch drinking a glass of wine.

"What have you done to me?" asked Trishka with her eyes closed. Ivan patted the back of Trishka's head and said.

"The chip in there contains all the information needed to make the brain for another K Fifty Five computer and it also allows the brain in the existing K Fifty Five in the United States to continue functioning. You are going to make me very, very rich, Trishka." Ivan walked to the door, then stopped, turned around and said.

"If anyone tries to take that chip out without first discussing the details with me, you'll die a horrible slow, painful death so keep your mouth shut!"

Trishka didn't doubt for a second that what Ivan said wasn't truthful because during the years of working for him as his secretary she heard numerous conversations he had with dangerous Russian party members and she knew Ivan was not a person to antagonize or she would suffer the consequences. He left her apartment, went down the stairs to his car and drove to his apartment. After Ivan finished eating dinner he walked to a covered device on top of a cabinet in the corner of his living room and lifted the cover. Ivan built the machine and knew that it would convert the flashing red box into a different format that would look innocent. He was glad that he had thought of doing what he was about to do to protect himself. The machine that was under the cover looked like a waffle maker. He took some filmy plastic material out of a drawer, inserted it and the flashing red box into the machine and pressed a button on the machine. Ivan went into the kitchen and poured himself a glass of wine, then went back to the machine and waited until he heard it beep, then opened it. The flashing box was gone and had changed into what looked like a regular music CD. He carefully lifted the fake CD out of the machine and while walking back to the kitchen almost tripped on a small rug. He looked at the fake CD in his hand and said out loud.

"If I dropped you, you'd shatter and I'd lose all the information inside. That's why I'm glad I had a copy of all the information deposited in Trishka's skull."

Ivan held the device close to his chest, then put it in his jacket pocket. The next morning, Ivan drove his car to a bridge over a river. He parked next to the bridge and got out of his car as a small truck drove up and stopped. A young man in a suit got out of the truck and walked over to Ivan.

"Are you Ivan Sakalov?" Ivan shook his head "yes".

"Vladimir sent me for the computer information" said the man.

"I want to see some money first" said Ivan. The man looked upset.

"Fuck you. Give me the box. Vladimir didn't tell me to give you any money". Ivan reached into his jacket and pulled out a pistol.

"Here it is". Ivan shot the man in the chest three times, killing him. He picked up the man's body and pushed it down the hill into the river. Then Ivan walked to his car and drove back to his apartment. Ivan sat down on the couch and picked up a book to read. His cell phone began ringing and he clicked it on, Vladimir Mikhail was sitting at his desk in his office. His huge hand was wrapped around his telephone receiver. He was watching an ant making its way toward the desk top. Yuri was standing by the window. Vladimir was holding a small tape recorder to his phone. Ivan was listening to his cell phone. All of a sudden he heard a voice coming from his phone. It was a recording of the voice of the man he shot.

"Are you Ivan Sakalov? Vladimir sent me for the computer information."

"I want to see some money first"

"Fuck you. Give me the box. Vladimir didn't tell me to give you any money".

"Here it is".

Then Ivan heard the gun shots he fired at the man. Vladimir said to Ivan on the phone.

"Mischa's dead body was floating in the river."

Vladimir squished the ant against the desk with his thumb and said.

"But my brother Yuri found his tape recorder in the bushes where it must have fallen".

Ivan pulled the phone away from his ear and his face was frozen with fear. He could hardly speak.

"Via . . . Vladimir?" Vladimir yelled into his telephone.

"You thought you could double cross us? You piece of shit ,..soon you'll be a memory."

Ivan's hand was shaking as he said into his telephone.

"Please Vladimir. All I wanted was some money for what I did for you." Vladimir threw his telephone receiver against the wall. Ivan closed his phone. His face was alive with total terror. His mouth drooped.

Trishka was asleep on her couch. She woke up when she heard constant banging on the door. She stumbled to the door.

"Who's there?"

"It's Ivan. Open the door, Trishka!"

The door was shaking as Ivan kept kicking it. Trishka unlocked the door and Ivan rushed in.

"Give me your car keys. I saw Vladimir and his brother following me. I have to get away!" A car pulls up outside. Vladimir and Yuri are inside. Ivan looks out the window and sees them get out of the car. He goes for Trishka's purse and she pulls it towards her. Paper money, keys and other things fly out. Ivan shoves her. She falls forward and the front of her head hits the side of a table. Her passport drops from the table to the floor on the side of the couch. Trishka sinks down against the wall. Ivan grabs her car keys and runs out. Trishka moans and crawls to the money scattered on the floor. She starts picking it up and shoves it into her purse. She doesn't notice the passport next to the couch. Ivan comes out the back door of the apartment building and Yuri's standing there with a gun pointed at him. Vladimir's car is right behind Yuri and Vladimir is sitting in the driver's seat. Yuri whispers something in Ivan's ear and Ivan says, "She's in apartment 203." Vladimir gets out of the car and opens the trunk. Then he picks Ivan up, throws him in the trunk and slams it shut. Trishka had been watching all the action below from her bedroom window. She sees Yuri pointing up to her apartment. She hurries to the front door, opens it and runs down the hall. Yuri and Vladimir go to Trishka's apartment. Vladimir picks the lock and they begin searching the rooms. Yuri spots a passport next to the couch. He picks it up and shows Vladimir Trishka's picture.

"She's Ivan's secretary. Her friend Lena works for my friend Alexei a computer programmer right next to Ivan's office."

Vladimir looks at Trishka's picture.

"Ask your friend Alexei where Lena lives. I'm sure she'll tell us where to find Trishka Perova".

Vladimir is driving the car and Yuri is in the passenger seat next to him. They are heading down a dirt road in the beautiful countryside. Vladimir pulls up next to a small cottage. Yuri gets out, opens the trunk and grabs Ivan, who is shaking like a leaf as Yuri carries him inside the cottage and ties him to a chair in the living room. Vladimir is smiling and stroking Ivan's head.

Ivan is sweating, his eyes are wide open with fear. Vladimir says in a soft voice.

"Where is the box with the computer information?" Ivan is terrified. He can't believe what is happening.

"Soon they'll find out that I blew up the Tverskaya Building and destroyed the K Fifty Five computer. Please, Vladimir I beg you. Give me some money so I can leave Russia." Vladimir looks down at Ivan.

"I'll ask you one more time Ivan. Where is the box?" Ivan looks up at Vladimir who takes Ivan's head gently between his huge hands and runs a finger up and down Ivan's neck.

"The human neck is especially weak. Did you know that Ivan?"

Ivan reaches in his jacket pocket, takes out the fake CD and hands it to Vladimir.

"I made this from the box." Ivan says. Ivan hopes that Vladimir will let him tell how he transformed the box into the fake CD. Instead

Vladimir snarls, then yells at Ivan.

"Do you think I'm stupid?" Ivan slams the CD against the wall and it falls to the floor in hundreds of pieces. Then Vladimir snaps Ivan's head, breaking his neck.

Lena Cheka is sitting at her piano in her apartment playing a Bach fugue. She is an excellent piano player in her late twenties with long black hair and brown eyes. She is concentrating on her piano playing and at first does not hear the knocking on her front door.

"Lena. It's Trishka. Open the door! "Lena stops playing, gets up and opens the door. Trishka rushes in, panic stricken.

"Trish . . . what's the matter!" Trishka sobs.

"They killed Ivan!"

"The Solntsevos?" asks Lena.

"It was on the news this morning, Lena. The police found Ivan's body floating in the river."

"He must have betrayed them".

"I've got to leave Russia, Lena. The Solvtsevos will be looking for me now. I've lost my passport. What can I do?"

Trishka and Lena are almost the same age. Lena opens a drawer in her desk, takes out her passport and hands it to Trishka.

"Use mine, and from now on you must speak English like my father taught you to do. You look tired. Lie down and take a nap. When you wake up we'll dye your hair".

Trishka kissed Lena on the cheek, then laid down on the living room couch. Before she drifted off to sleep, Trishka remembered when she and Lena were young girls living with their parents in rented houses in the country on the outskirts of Moscow. Almost every Sunday Lena's parents had Trishka and her parents over to their house for dinner. Lena's father was a high school teacher and he taught both Lena and Trishka how to speak perfect English. Lena also started taking piano lessons when she was eleven. When Lena was seventeen, her parents and eight other Russian loyalists were killed by Chechen separatists while they were attending a political meeting in Moscow. After that, Trishka's parents took Lena in and she and Trishka became as close as sisters. Then, a year later, tragedy struck again. Trishka's parents were killed when a drunken driver smashed into their car. Lena went to live with an aunt, and Trishka joined the Russian Army. After she finished her tour of duty, Trishka answered Ivan's ad for a secretary who spoke English and he hired her on the spot. Trishka then helped Lena get a job working for a computer programmer in the office next to Ivan's. Lena came to Moscow and found the small apartment where she currently lives. Lena is drying Trishka's hair which has been dyed black. Lena opens a small container and shows Trishka two brown contact lenses.

"I got these at a pharmacy while you were sleeping."

Lena helps Trishka put the contact lenses into Trishka's eyes. They now look like twins.

"I'll miss your concert." "I know Trish . . . but you have to leave Russia".

Lena helps Trishka pack her suitcase and get ready for her trip. They are standing at Lena's front door. Lena writes something on a piece of paper and hands it to Trishka.

"It's the address of a Russian nightclub in Los Angeles, Trish and from now on, only speak English, not Russian, don't forget".

"Ok, I won't."

Doctor Gorchakov is sleeping in bed in a Moscow hospital. An oxygen mask covers his nose and mouth. The entire top of his head is bandaged covering the injury inflicted on him by Ivan with the soldering iron. Vladimir and Yuri both dressed as hospital orderlies are standing over him. Vladimir unhooks the oxygen mask and pulls it off, waking him up. Vladimir holds a business card in front of Gorchakov's eyes.

"We found this in Ivan's pocket. What did he want?" Doctor Gorchakov just stares at Vladimir. Then Vladimir yells.

"You work for us Gorchakov. Now I'll ask you one more time . . . what did Ivan want with you?!" The doctor in a shakey whisper says.

"Ivan brought a woman to my office. He had me inject something into the back of her head." Vladimir is extremely disturbed. He speaks loudly right in Gorchakov's face.

"What does she look like!" Gorchakov's hands are shaking as he whispers to Vladimir.

"Young, blue eyes, blond hair." Vladimir takes out Trishka's passport and shows him her picture. Gorchakov shakes his head "yes".

"You've been here more than a week and you wouldn't have told us anything if we didn't find your card in Ivan's pocket, would you!?"

Gorchakov's hands continue to shake. He is totally frightened as he stares at Vladimir. Vladimir gives Yuri a hand signal. Yuri takes the pillow from under Gorchakov's head and smothers him until he flat lines, then Yuri puts the pillow back under Gorvhakov's head and replaces the oxygen mask. Vladimir and Yuri immediately go into the hall and out the exit before anyone sees them.

CHAPTER 3

FBI agent Rick Jubas is sitting behind his desk in his office on the seventeenth floor of the Federal Building in Westwood, California. It's nine a.m. and FBI agent John Mason, good looking, thirties, comes in. "Good morning John".

"Morning Rick". I want to show you what's on this DVD I just received from our Russian contact."

Jubas turns off the lights and pushes a button on his DVD player then points to the giant television screen in the corner of the room.

Images of men standing in front of a building appear on the screen. They are all wearing T-shirts. Jubas says.

"Notice that none of them have their uniforms on. That's because no one is supposed to know that they are in the Russian military."

Jubas zooms in on Vladimir, short hair, clean shaven, tattoos up and down each arm and on his neck and shoulders. Jubas point to him and says.

"That's Vladimir Mikhail. Intelligent, cunning, ruthless. He speaks flawless English. He headed an elite Russian torture squad a few years ago in Georgia. The Russians wanted to stop Georgia from breaking away from Russia and becoming part of NATO." Jubas zooms in on Yuri, long messy hair, a beard also with tattoos on his arms, neck and shoulders. Jubas says. "That's Vladimir's brother, Yuri." Then John asks. "Who are the rest of the men?"

"We don't know who they are, but they're standing in front of a grammar school in Russian Georgia. Now watch the ugliness that was recorded with a hidden school camera."

Jubas pushes the fast forward button on the DVD player. A horrible scene appears on the television screen of many dead bodies strewn across the lawn in front of the school. Pictures of the men including Vladimir and Yuri are standing by the front door of the school building holding pistols, laughing.

"The Mikhail brothers and the other men murdered those twenty five school teachers after they heard that the teachers were discussing with their students why Georgia should become part of NATO. I know for a fact that the Mikhail brothers are top dogs in the Solntsevos, the biggest Russian mafia gang in Moscow. Now the Solntsevos are trying to infiltrate the Longshoremen's Union in Long Beach so they can ship drugs into the U.S. which would make them billions of dollars a year. If they can get that kind of money from the Longshoremen's Union they will be able to create fictitious companies to evade payment of excise taxes when they sell gasoline and diesel fuel from gas stations they purchase in and around Los Angeles and the taxes charged to the customers will be skimmed and sent to offshore banks rather than being forwarded to federal and state taxing authorities. The Solntsevos have done these kinds of things in Brighton Beach, and they've been getting away with it for years. We don't want anything like that happening in California, John".

Jubas fast forwards the DVD player and freezes on a building with large words on the wall "AMERICAN-RUSSIAN SOCIAL CLUB".

"It's the Russian mob's main hang out. The place is in downtown Los Angeles and is owned by a Russian, Serge Koszmakoff. We think he's one of the big shots in the Russian mafia, in fact he may be the head of the organization in America, but we can't prove it and we think he ordered the death of the prior owner because the guy wouldn't sell the building to him, but the LAPD couldn't find the car that killed the owner nor could they find any witnesses who would say a word against Kozmakoff." John scratches his head and says.

"Yeah, I remember being at an interrogation session as a government representative and the whole thing was a waste of time."

"You know John that if someone testifies against the Russian mafia, they'll tear that person's guts out."

"After his death the guy's wife sold the place to Koszmakoff. The DA questioned her, but all she would say was she didn't want the place any longer. But I'll bet the real reason was she didn't want to die."

John looks at Jubas and shakes his head "yes".

"John, you're half Russian and you speak the language".

"Yeah . . . so?"

"Well, tonight you're gonna start doing a little spying there. Our Russian contact told us that the Mikhail brothers might be coming to Los Angeles and chances are they'll visit that Russian club." John doesn't look happy. He had planned to take his son to the movies after work.

"The club uses under age girls, illegals, dopers, anything with a pussy to make a buck, John. We also think Serge Koszmakoff finds Russian women in Los Angeles who have green cards or permanent residence permits and pays them thousands of dollars to marry Russian mafia members which allows the members to legally stay in the United States. We've questioned dozens of the Russian women and they all say they married for love, so it's very difficult to prove any illegality. Your job John, is to mix with the people in the club and see if you can get to the bottom of any illegal activities, but the most important thing for you to do is to locate the Mikhail brothers because if they get a foothold in Los Angeles they will really cause problems for this country. If you see either of them let me know immediately and I'll pass it on to DC. Don't bring your gun to the club, because they search everybody that comes in."

That night, John parks his car across the street from a ramshackle graffiti covered downtown Los Angeles building with neon lights on the wall flashing "AMERICAN-RUSSIAN SOCIAL CLUB. He turns off his headlights, gets out of the car and walks into the club.

Serge Koszmakoff is sitting on a couch in his office which is right above the nightclub. Loud Russian music filters through the walls and floor. Trishka is standing next to him. He leers at Trishka's smooth silky legs under her soft chiffon dress.

"I own this club and get half of what the girls make here."

Trishka shakes her head "yes".

"Good, then you'll start tonight".

Downstairs in the club, men and women are standing around laughing, talking in English and Russian. John is sitting at the bar. He's wearing Levis and cowboy boots. Trishka comes downstairs and sits on a barstool a few feet from John. A man with greasy hair and thick glasses sits next to Trishka. He's slopping French fries and ketchup. He says in broken English through a mouthful of food.

"You like go home with Boris?" A glop of ketchup drops from his chin. Trishka wipes it off her arm. John watches as she gets up and goes to the end of the bar. A pretty woman walks over to John. She puts her hand on his leg.

"How about some sex?" John shakes his head "no" and leans toward the bartender.

"I'll have a Bud Light". The woman comes close to John and whispers.

"You want a blow job?" John shakes his head again.

"No thanks."

The bartender pops the top off the beer and hands it to John. The woman makes a face, walks away and sits next to another man. John sees Trishka go out the front door. He shrugs his shoulders and starts drinking the beer. Suddenly he turns in the direction of yelling coming from outside the building. Trishka is standing outside at the bus stop. Boris is yelling at her.

"I said you come with Boris!" He grabs her. She shoves back. John walks up.

"The lady wants to be left alone." Boris turns.

"You know what means fuck you mister?"

John steps between Boris and Trishka. Boris shoves him. John knows he could easily break the guy's neck but he holds back and says.

"You shouldn't have done that fatso."

Boris tries to touch Trishka's breasts. John starts toward Boris. But before he reaches him, Trishka slams her right elbow into Boris' face, then pokes him in the eyes with her fingers. Boris goes down, blood streaming from his nose. Then he stumbles to his feet, puts up his hands in submission and slowly walks away. John looks amazed.

"Where did you learn to fight like that?"

Trishka remains silent. A bus pulls up and she gets in. She smiles at John from inside and mouths the word "Thanks".

Vladimir and Yuri are inside Lena's apartment in Moscow. They have her tied to a piano leg and speak to her in Russian.

"Where is Trishka?" asks Yuri. Lena just stares at him. Vladimir gently strokes her hands. Then whispers delicately in her ear.

"You're going to be the guest pianist at a concert at the conservatory next week aren't you Lena?"

He strokes her hands again.

"And you wouldn't want anything unpleasant to happen to your ability to play the piano would you?"

She stares wide eyed at Vladimir and shakes her head. His big hand squeezes her neck. While his other hand is still stroking her hands he says softly.

"Then tell us where we can find Trishka Perova".

Lena looks terror stricken. Her whole life revolves around her piano playing so when Vladimir bends down, Lena whispers something in his ear. He smiles, looks over at Yuri and motions to him. Yuri comes over with a pair of pliers and a baseball bat. He hands the bat to Vladimir, who says to Lena.

"You should have told me sooner". Yuri grabs one of Lena's fingers with the pliers and Vladimir raises the bat above her head. She screams.

CHAPTER 4

United States President William Farley walks around the Oval Office of the White House while he's talking on his cell phone to Russian President Chernov.

"I know that President Chernov, but we would have to make another K Fifty Five computer here in Washington, then ship it to you in Russia".

Farley listens to what President Chernov says. Then Farley says to President Chernov.

"First, mister President, we must take all the coding information from our K Fifty Five which I will have done immediately. Good day sir".

Vice President Roger Ames comes in. Farley is looking out a window. President Farley hasn't told Ames about the K Fifty Five computers yet but now feels it's time to do so.

"Roger, you know how hard President Chernov and I have tried to stop rogue countries from nuclear testing. Well so far nothing's worked and the whole thing has gotten out of hand. I want you to promise that you will not speak a word of what I'm going to tell you to anyone".

"I promise sir."

"At Langley Air Force Base, I have caused to be developed what is known as the K Fifty Five Super Computer. With it, we'll be able to use radio and television transmissions and every other method in existence, to totally neutralize nuclear devices of any kind and nature whatsoever on this planet at the speed of light".

"But sir, what about the countries that use atomic energy for peaceful purposes?"

"I have a list of each country that uses nuclear power for peaceful purposes and those countries will not be affected by our shutting down and neutralizing non peaceful nuclear devices, unless of course, a country's purported peaceful use of nuclear power is a lie".

"I understand, mister President".

"Roger, the construction of the two super computers took us over six months and over ten thousand man hours to build. Each person who worked on the computers did only what his or her job called for and did not know what any of the other workers were doing. Sidney Manning, the computer genius was in total control of the operation. That way I was assured that no one knew the full impact of those computers and what they were designed for unless and until I told who I wanted to tell. I let the Russians borrow one of them at the urgent request of President Chernov, but terrorists blew it up a few days ago. So now we have the only K Fifty Five in existence. I'm sorry I didn't tell you sooner, Roger but I kept it totally top secret. I haven't informed the National Security Council, the CIA or the FBI except for one agent, Rick Jubas with whom I spent four years in the Marines in the hills of Afghanistan. That's because, as you must know I can't trust everyone working for our government. I want you to realize that only a few people including you, Russian President Chernov, General Starker, Rick Jubas and our computer genius Sidney Manning know anything about the K Fifty Five operation and I want to keep it that way. Ivan Sakalov who worked for President Chernov knew about the K Fifty Five, but my understanding is that the

Russian mafia killed him because he refused to tell them how the K Fifty Five worked".

President Farley grasps both of Ames' shoulders and looks him in the eyes.

"Roger, if this secret operation went public, I'd probably be forced to resign as President. However, I'll take my chances, because I feel it's worth it for the safety of our country. You're the Vice President and I want you to know that I've put all of the information about the K Fifty Five in my safe for you in case something should happen to me".

Vice President Ames looks amazed. He salutes the President and says.

"Thank you for telling me about the K Fifty Five mister President. I promise that it will remain a secret with me sir".

President Farley puts his hand over his chest.

"I thank you from my heart, Roger. Now we have to decide whether to build a second K Fifty Five and send it to President Chernov to replace the one that was destroyed, because he periodically becomes aware of governments that would not hesitate to use nuclear devices against us if the timing is right and I trust the man because of what he did for me".

"May I ask what that was sir?"

"President Chernov is the one who saved the lives of thirty five of our soldiers the Afghans were holding and would have killed if Chernov hadn't released ten Afghan hostages the Russians had captured after I asked him to. My brother Charles was one of our thirty five soldiers President Chernov saved."

Sidney Manning the computer genius and General Samuel Starker a tall man in uniform are standing next to a carbon copy of the K Fifty Five computer that Ivan destroyed in Moscow. Manning and Starker are each holding a key which they insert into locks on a safe next to the computer. The safe door opens and Manning takes out a small box and puts it on a shelf inside the computer.

"I'm ready general". Starker steps back.

"Go ahead Manning".

Manning types something on the keyboard. Lights come on and the computer hums. Manning turns to Starker.

"It's done, sir". Manning takes out the small box but it's not flashing red. He shakes his head and hands it to Starker who looks at it in wide eyed amazement.

President Farley is sitting behind his desk when General Starker enters the Oval Office.

"Good morning Sam."

"Good day, Mister President."

"Did everything go as planned?"

"No sir, it hasn't". Starker opens his briefcase, takes out the small box and hands it to Farley.

"Something's gone wrong sir. It's supposed to be flashing red which would mean it contained all the essential information to construct another K Fifty Five computer. However, it appears to be dead".

"What do you mean, General?"

"For some unknown reason, it can't retrieve the computer's information, and if the information can't be retrieved, then we won't be able to build another K Fifty Five. Worse than that Mister President, the K Fifty

Five we have is no longer operative".

"What!"

"At this moment sir, Sidney Manning who as you know is probably the finest computer genius in America and maybe the world, is checking it out".

President Farley is extremely upset.

"I want to be advised of Manning's progress every day!"

"Yes sir".

Starker leaves the Oval Office and President Farley frowns, then flops down in his chair.

CHAPTER 5

John and Trishka are sitting at a table in the corner of the Russian club. He finishes his beer and they get up, walk out of the club and get into his car. She gets in the front passenger seat and he starts the engine and turns on the headlights. She gently pokes him in the shoulder.

"I'm staying at a hotel in Hollywood".

John and Trishka are in her hotel room. Soft music can be heard in the background. There is no furniture except a single bed and two chairs. Trishka is standing next to John holding a bottle of beer. He takes off his jacket and tosses it on a chair. John feels very protective of Trishka for some reason.

"I've got a bit of friendly advice for you".

"What?"

"You should find a different job."

"Why?"

"Come on. It's a goddam whorehouse!"

John stands up and picks up his jacket. His wallet falls out open on the chair. Trishka glances at it and sees John's FBI card.

"You're an FBI agent?"

John shakes his head "yes". Trishka goes to her front door, opens it and motions to John with her hand to leave. He picks up a piece of paper, writes on it and hands it to her.

"It's my cell phone number". Trishka keeps the paper in her hand, but just stares coldly at John.

"Please leave."

John walks out with a sad look on his face. Trishka slams the door and John gets into his car and drives off into the night.

Trishka is standing in the hotel room in her underwear. She picks up the hotel phone and dials.

Lena is lying in a hospital bed in Moscow, with her hands bandaged. A nurse is holding a telephone and says in Russian, "It's Trishka Perova." Lena is sobbing. She speaks to Trishka in Russian.

"He broke my fingers and hit me in the head with a baseball bat. I had to tell them where you are. One man called the other man Vladimir as they were leaving my apartment. Vladimir is big and scary. Be careful Trish, they know where you are."

The nurse hangs the phone up for Lena. Trishka hangs up the phone and begins to cry.

Trishka is sleeping on the bed. Someone knocks on her door. She gets up and wraps a blanket around her body.

"Who's there?"

"Rod, the building manager". Trishka opens the door and Rod looks her up and down.

"Your rent's late".

"I'll pay you".

"Sorry, I've already rented the place to someone else".

"You can't just throw me out!"

"Oh no? Where's your federal work permit, Ruskie".

Trishka is speechless. She knows that she'd be forced to leave the country if he reported her to the authorities and they checked her background. She just stares at Rod. Rod says, "I speak Russian and I heard you speaking Russian on the phone. I called the number back and the Russian nurse told me who you really are. You're name is

Trishka Perova and you're from Moscow aren't you?" Trishka doesn't respond. She looks down and the floor and begins to cry.

"I thought so. Now get out or I'll call immigration."

Rod stares at Trishka, then storms out of the room.

Trishka closes the door and drops to her knees on the floor. She bangs the floor with her fist, then sobs.

John is lying on his living room couch reading a paperback book. His cell phone rings. He clicks it on.

"Hello"

"John, it's Trishka from the club. I have to talk to you. I'm sorry I was rude can we meet?"

Later, John is cleaning his dirty kitchen. He picks up clothes on the floor and hangs them in the closet. He hears someone knock at the front door.

"Who's there?"

"It's Trishka". John opens the door. Trishka walks in. She's wearing a loose fitting T-shirt and shorts. Very sexy. John can't keep his eyes off her.

"I need your help."

"Why. What happened?"

"The building manager rented my room to someone else because I couldn't pay my rent. He found out I was Russian and threatened to call immigration".

"Hold on. You mean you're here illegally?"

Trishka looks panicky.

"The Russian mafia is after me so I had to leave Russia. I lost my passport and my friend let me have hers. I know you're an FBI agent, but I have nobody else to turn to".

"Why is the Russian mafia after you?"

"Please, John. Can I trust you?"

"First tell me why the Russian mafia is looking for you".

Trishka looks down at the floor.

"Trishka?" She looks up at John, wipes the tears from her eyes.

"It's two of their top men. It has something to do with the giant computer that was blown up by my Russian boss. Can I stay here for awhile?"

CHAPTER 6

Rick Jubas is sitting behind his desk in his FBI office. John is standing in front of the desk.

"Did she tell you who's looking for her?"

"Yeah, Rick. Two men in the Russian mafia, but she didn't mention names."

"I told you about Vladimir and Yuri Mikhail of the Russian mafia and the other day I showed you their pictures on that DVD. This morning I was told about their knowledge of the destruction of a giant secret Russian computer called the K Fifty Five. John, this entire situation is top secret per President Farley. Is that understood?"

"I understand, Rick".

"Good. Now he wants us to find the Mikhail brothers. If there's any way the girl you met can point us in their direction, make certain you follow up one hundred percent. Convince her to continue working at that Russian club. Keep her under your wing John so we can find the Mikhail brothers."

"What about her safety?" Jubas hesitates briefly.

"John, the security of our country is far more important than her safety. Just do what you can for her. Ok?"

John leaves the FBI headquarters and heads home behind the wheel of his car. He stares at the road ahead of him like he's in a daze, and almost rear ends a Porsche, but he slams on his brakes just in time. John parks his car and unlocks the front door of his house. Trishka is asleep on the couch covered with a blanket.

"Rise and shine pretty girl." Trishka opens her eyes and smiles at John.

"Thank you for letting me sleep here."

"You're welcome. Are you hungry?" Trishka shakes her head "yes".

"Do you have any eggs?"

"Yeah, in the fridge."

Trishka gets up. She's only wearing panties and her T-shirt. Her shorts are on a chair next to the couch. She looks down at her panties and goes back to the couch, grabs the blanket and covers herself. John has been staring at her and smiling. She looks embarrassed.

"I forgot that I undressed for bed. Will you get my shorts please?"

John takes her shorts off the chair and hands them to her. She puts them on while the blanket is covering her.

"I must be losing my mind."

"You don't have to apologize, you're beautiful."

John imagines how it would be making love to her as he goes to the refrigerator and takes out some eggs. Trishka still looks embarrassed. John hands her a frying pan and some butter. She goes to the stove and starts cooking the eggs. John puts his hands on her shoulders while she's stirring the eggs in the frying pan. Trishka turns around and looks up at him.

"What am I going to do about my job?" John recalls his conversation about Trishka with Jubas. He shrugs his shoulders.

"You told me to leave the place."

"I know, but I thought about it and I think you should stay there until something better comes along."

She looks away.

"Don't worry Trishka, you're safe with me."

Trishka gives John a hug. She closes her eyes. He looks very serious. While her eyes are closed, he holds her head in his hands and kisses her on the forehead. She pulls back when he touches the place where the doctor injected the chip. John takes his hands away from her head.

"What's wrong?" Trishka slowly rubs the back of her head.

"I've got a migraine, that's all." John looks down, then back at her.

"What part of Russia are you from Trish?"

"Kiev."

"My father was born in Kiev" John says in Russian.

Trishka looks surprised and excited.

"You speak Russian?" She says in Russian.

"Yes Trish. Ok if I call you Trish?" She shakes her head "yes".

"I must tell you something very important."

"What?"

"I'm undercover and we're looking for Vladimir and Yuri Mikhail, the same bastards who are looking for you."

Trishka begins to tremble. John wraps his arms around her, sits her down on the couch and stands next to her.

"I won't let them hurt you Trish."

"I've been using my friend's passport".

Trishka takes Lena's passport out of her purse and shows it to him.

"My hair is really blond and my eyes are blue. I dyed my hair black and have brown contact lenses so I could use the passport."

"Keep your hair dark and don't stop using the contact lenses. They will be looking for someone with blond hair and blue eyes. I'll get you a passport and California driver's license which will show you with black hair and brown eyes. But it's imperative that you don't tell anyone that I'm an FBI agent."

Trishka gently touches his arm

"I won't, I promise."

John looks down at her.

"I'll protect you, don't worry."

Trishka stands up, hugs John, then begins to cry.

"Trish, how did you learn to fight like I saw you do the other night?"

"I joined the Russian Army when I was eighteen. Right after my father and mother were killed in a car accident. I wanted to fight the Chechen pricks, but I was assigned to a desk job in Moscow. The captain of my unit was also a friend from high school. He told me about the Miss Russian Army Contest, which was being held a month after I joined the army. He said that I would have a good chance of winning, so I entered the contest."

John just stares at Trishka and smiles.

"I came in second and felt honored. Our unit went out that weekend to celebrate my victory. Then something horrible happened. While I was walking back to the barracks alone, I was dragged behind a building and raped by a soldier from another unit." John's face freezes.

"What did they do to him for that?"

"Nothing. I told my captain, but he said not to do anything, because the father of the soldier who raped me was very high up in the Russian government and if I went to the authorities, I would most likely be charged with lying about the rape and be blamed for the whole ordeal because the prick who raped me would say it was consensual. The captain said I could even be sent to prison if I opened my mouth about the incident, so I didn't report what happened. But I spent my evenings taking Krav Magna lessons from an instructor who used to be in the Mossad which is the Israeli Secret Service."

John punches one of his hands with the other one and looks out the window.

"I'm well acquainted with the Mossad. I took Krav Magna lessons for three years." John looks back at Trishka as she continues.

"Krav Magna taught me how to disable and kill with my hands. After my Krav Magna training I kept my eyes on the son of a bitch who raped me. He would walk alone to his barracks through a park each night after he finished work. Then, one night when it was really dark I was ready for him. I was wearing jeans and a hoody which covered most of my head, so I could have been mistaken for a man. I walked up behind him in the deserted park, grabbed him and smashed him in the face. I felt blood gush onto my hand. Then I hit him in the mouth with my fist. He tried to defend himself, but I threw him to the ground and kicked him over and over in the balls. I grabbed his wallet, kicked him in the face and left him lying there. On my way back to my barracks I tossed his wallet into a sewer. I found out later that I'd broken his nose and knocked out five of his teeth. The police investigated the incident and concluded that it was probably done by a Russian gang member for the guy's money."

John takes her in his arms and says.

"Funny how things work out,"

She kisses him.

"You can stay here until I find you an apartment of your own."

She kisses him again.

"Thank you John".

He tickles her and smiles.

"You're very welcome. Incidentally, where did you learn to speak English so well?"

"My friend's father was a high school teacher in Russia. He taught English, that's how I learned".

CHAPTER 7

John and the master computer technician Sidney Manning from Washington DC are sitting at a table in a Starbucks in Westwood Village having morning coffee.

"I'm sorry about your mom, Sid". Sidney has tears in his eyes. "The doctor said she's only going to live a couple more days. The cancer has eaten her up. They put her in a drug induced coma because of her pain. General Starker let me come to Los Angeles to see her before she dies."

John puts his hand on Sidney's wrist. "Is there anything I can do for you Sid?" "No John, I owe you my life. Remember?"

When Sidney was nine and John was ten they went swimming at a YMCA in the San Fernando Valley. John came out of the men's room saw Sidney floating under the pool surface. John jumped in and pulled Sidney out and began giving him CPR. Later, Sidney was lying on a stretcher on the pool deck and his mother was sitting on the floor next to him. The medic who was putting an oxygen mask on Sidney, pointed to John and looked over at Sidney's mother.

"That boy saved your son's life". Sidney's mother got up crying and looked into John's eyes.

"Sidney is all I have left in the world. I don't know how to thank you John, you are my savior."

Sidney puts his coffee cup down.

"If it wasn't for you, I would have died that day. You're my best friend. Can you come to my mom's funeral?"

"Of course I will Sid." Sidney sobs.

"Thank you".

"How's the job going?"

"I've got so much on my plate. You wouldn't believe what

General Starker is having me do about our computer problems in DC."

John's cell phone rings. He clicks it on.

"Ok Rick I'll see you in a few minutes."

John gets up, goes over to Sidney and gives him a hug.

"Duty calls Sid. Just tell me when . . . you know."

"The funeral John".

They shake hands, and John walks out of Starbucks.

John is driving west on Wilshire Boulevard. He parks his car, gets out and goes into the Federal Building. He gets in the elevator and pushes 17. There are no other people in the elevator so it races up to the seventeenth floor and stops. The door opens and John walks down to Rick Jubas' office. Jubas is sitting at his desk. He hands John a large manila envelope.

"It's a passport and driver's license for Trishka Perova. Her name is now Nancy Stenson. I want you to find her an apartment, preferably in Studio City. When you find a suitable place, lease it and the FBI will pay the rent. There are quite a few Russians living in Studio City and besides it's close to your house in Sherman Oaks."

John is driving down Ventura Boulevard listening to classical music. He turns left on Woodman, drives a few blocks, then stops in front of his house. He gets out of the car holding the envelope that Jubas gave him and goes into the house. Trishka is standing there.

"I have something for you Trish." He hands her the envelope and she takes out what's inside.

"Oh my God. A passport and driver's license and my name is now Nancy Stenson?" She laughs.

"Yeah . . . Nancy." He laughs.

"We'll find you an apartment in Studio City. We'll look for one tomorrow. Now let's go outside".

John and Trishka are standing next to a white ten year old Toyota that's parked in front of John's house. John hands Trishka a set of keys. "It's yours." "The car's for me?" "So is this."

John takes a cell phone out of his jacket.

"It's disposable so no one can trace your calls." ·

Trishka stares at the car and the phone then gives John a long hug.

They stand in front the the house holding each other for awhile.

"I don't know how to thank you."

John smiles and spanks her butt gently.

"Thank the FBI Trish". She laughs.

He walks back to the house and goes inside. Trishka gets into the Toyota and closes the door. Then she clicks the cell phone on and dials. She puts the phone to her ear and it just rings. Finally an a voice from an answering machine can be heard and it finally goes silent. "Lena, it's Trishka. I . . ."

Suddenly someone answers the phone in Russian. Trishka pulls the phone away from her ear then puts it back.

"Missus Cheka?" It's Lena's aunt on the other end of the line crying.

"Trishka, Lena died yesterday".

Trishka is totally distraught. She sobs. Her voice shakes as she speaks in Russian.

"How did she die?"

Lena's aunt answers in Russian.

"A brain concussion from her head wounds."

Tears roll down Trishka's face as she drops her phone.

CHAPTER 8

John and Rick Jubas are at an indoor pistol range in Glendale. They are both wearing ear muffs and are standing at a counter looking a the paper target of a man's head surrounded by a black circle hanging down about one hundred feet in front of them. Jubas points his pistol at the target and fires. The bullet hits just inside the black circle and misses the man's head completely. He shoots again the bullet barely hits the edge of the black circle.

"Shit. Your turn".

John shoots at the target and the bullet hits the man's face right between the eyes. He shoots again and the second bullet hits the man's face about one inch away from the first shot. He shoots a third time and the bullet hits the man's face right next to the first two shots.

"Christ, John that's fantastic. The only other shooter that was as good as you was Jelly Bryce, the FBI's greatest sharpshooter".

"That was in nineteen twenty five, Jubas."

"So what. You're a better shot than anyone I know. Why don't you carry your Glock 23 instead of that 38 Special?"

"Because the Glock is much bigger than the 38 and I can hide the 38 in my pocket. Besides, I only use Plus-P ammo and you know what that can do to someone's head, hopefully to whoever killed my wife!"

"Just keep things legal, ok? By the way did you pay your NRA dues this year?" John smirks.

"I'm a lifetime member".

"How's your son doing John?"

"Well, after the guy killed Sara, Sam's aunt Angela has been taking care of him at her house in West Hollywood." Jubas pats John on the back.

"Sam really was lucky that day Rick. He was able to hide under his bed and the killer left after he killed Sara. If the guy would've looked under the bed he would've killed Sam too. Thank God he didn't. The cops never caught the prick. That's the main reason I quit the Secret Service and joined the FBI. I wanted to be in Los Angeles close to my son instead of working in DC. One of these days I'll find the fucker who killed Sara and blow his head off."

"I wouldn't blame you if you did, John. But as I said, keep things legal." John lowers his eyes and shakes his head "yes".

"I'm taking Sam out on my boat this weekend. He's twelve years old and time really flies. Before you know it, he'll be grown up and that's why I want to spend as much time with him as my job will allow."

"How's Angela doing with him?" John smiles.

"She's the best Rick. That's why I give her a big chunk of my paycheck each month. I'll do anything to keep my son safe and happy." Jubas' cell phone rings and he clicks it on.

"No mister President, I haven't discussed the matter with him yet."

Jubas listens to what the President says to him on the phone.

"Yes sir, I would trust Mason with my life."

Jubas shuts the cell phone, looks over at John and whispers to him.

"That was President Farley. There's something I must tell you as soon as we get back to my office."

"We can't talk here?"

Jubas looks around the pistol range at the other shooters. Then shakes his head "no" and again whispers to John.

"No, John. It's top secret and it's very important."

They take off their ear muffs and sign out on the pistol range register. Then they walk out the door and they go to their cars.

Jubas is sitting behind his desk in his office on his telephone.

"Thank you mister President. I'll discuss the matter with Mason as soon as he gets here."

Jubas hangs up the phone, walks to his door and opens it. John is waiting outside in the hall.

"Come in John."

John walks over to the couch and sits down.

"President Farley advised me that Vladimir and Yuri Mikhail, the Russian brothers we're after are working for the Russian government and have diplomatic immunity. He also said that they're after Trishka Perova whom you are protecting."

"Yeah . . . she told me those Russian scumbags were looking for her, but why do they want her?"

"Apparently she was secretary to Ivan Sakalov, the guy who destroyed the Russian K Fifty Five computer that Farley let president Chernov use and the Mikhal brothers want to find out if she knows if Sakalov made a memory box of the computer's brain before he blew up the computer and if so, what happened to the memory box. If Sakalov made that box and it was destroyed then not only can't another K Fifty Five be made, but our K Fifty Five would be useless".

"What's the big deal about these computers, Rick?"

"I don't know John. President Farley didn't tell me and I didn't want to ask . . . and . . . John, there's something else. I think you may be upset about what I'm going to tell you, but the order came directly from President Farley."

John looks worried.

"What's that Rick?"

"Farley wants you to resign from the FBI."
John now looks dumfounded.

"Resign . . . but why?"

"Remember I told you this whole affair was
top secret?"

John shakes his head "yes".

"Well, if you are no longer an official member
of the FBI and you have one or both of the
Mikhail brothers under your control, then . . ."

John stops Jubas in mid sentence.

"Then I wouldn't be bound by the diplomatic
immunity restrictions and I'd be able to force
whoever I had to spill the beans by any method
available to me?"

"But you'd be in serious trouble if you were
caught doing something illegal and you might
even end up in prison if it was serious enough,
and no government official would be able to help
you."

"Couldn't Farley pardon me?"

"Yes he could. President Farley knows that he
owes you his life. He would have been killed if

you hadn't shot Manuel Gomez before he tossed that grenade at Farley.

But before he pardoned you, he would have to carefully examine the entire situation. So it would be best if you kept things legal."

"What about my salary?"

"You'll be paid in cash. But you can't tell anyone about any of this. Just tell Sam's aunt that you've resigned from the FBI but you'll continue paying her for watching him out of your retirement fund."

"I'll do whatever Farley wants me to do."

"I'll get you a concealed weapons permit so you'll be able to legally carry your pistols after you leave the FBI".

General Starker is standing in front of President Farley's desk in the Oval Office and Farley is sitting behind the desk in his large leather chair.

"Well Starker, do you have any news about the problems with the K Fifty Five?"

"Mister President, we've discovered that the brain of our K Fifty Five computer has shut down because someone took the essential information

73

from the Russian K Fifty Five that was in a small metal box in that computer's safe. The metal box sent out radio waves which entered the brain of our K Fifty Five."

"I don't understand general."

"As I told you sir, if something happened to the memory of the Russian K Fifty Five, it would affect the operation of our K Fifty Five."

"But our K Fifty Five was fine yesterday, wasn't it?"

"Something must have happened to the metal box that we were tracking in Russia. Remember I told you that our special GPS showed us that someone took the box to a small village in northern Russia?"

"Yes and I called President Chernov who told me his people were going to retrieve it for us".

"It's not there anymore sir. We think it's been destroyed because there are no longer any signals coming from the place where the box was".

"You mean the information no longer exists?"

"We're not sure what happened sir but when the information was lost, it caused our K Fifty Five's brain to freeze."

"So we're back where we started. I guess we'll have to go to work right away and make another computer".

"It's worse than that sir. At least then we had the raw materials to build the original K Fifty Five. Now we no longer have those materials, because they were compressed into the metal box taken from the Russian computer. So we're dead in the water."

"What can we do Starker?"

"I have Sidney Manning our computer expert working to find an answer, mister President."

CHAPTER 9

Serge Koszmakoff is standing next to Aleks Misostov in Kosmakoff's office above the Russian club. Serge hands Misostov a drink and speaks to him in broken English.

"Aleks, I understand that Vladimir and Yuri Mikhail are coming to America very soon. How do they plan to get here when the FBI is looking for them?"

"You know they got me out of trouble, perhaps even prison in Moscow by pinning the crime I committed on a Serbian spy, and doing that made me look like a hero. Then I made a lot of money in the crude oil business before coming to America, so I owe them a lot."

"Yes Aleks, I know."

"I'm bringing both Mikhail and Yuri to the Palm Springs Airport in my private jet. I got both of them plus the other Russian men who are coming with them diplomatic passports and visas with third party names, which was approved by the Russian Federation because both Vladimir and Yuri and their fellow passengers have strong ties to important higher ups in Russia. All of them will have diplomatic immunity and will be safe in the United States.

The Gulfstream 550 is slowing down, preparing to land. Vladimir and Yuri are both in the airplane's restroom. Both men have their shirts off. Vladimir is almost finished washing the tattoos off Yuri's arms, shoulders and neck. The tattoos that appeared on Vladimir are completely gone.

"I'm almost finished getting rid of your tattoos, Yuri. Thanks for getting rid of mine".

"You're welcome, Vladimir. Jaska is the finest fake tattoo painter in all of Moscow. He did a great job on us." Yuri looks at himself in the mirror and sees that all his tattoos are gone.

"Yes. He thanked me for the extra money I gave him for the excellent removable tattoo work he did on us Yuri and I also warned him not to tell anyone about it". Vladimir looks at himself in the mirror. He now has long hair and a beard and Yuri has shaved the hair off his head and has a mustache.

"Maybe we should give ourselves fake American names. That way we'll be able to pick up American women easier. You could call yourself Victor instead of Vladimir and I could be Teddy instead of Yuri". They look at each other and both laugh. They now look totally different from the way they looked in Russia.

Three black limousines are parked near the Palm Springs Airport. The Gulfstream comes in for a landing. Vladimir, Yuri and the other men come down the stairway from the airplane. They show the TSA agent at the bottom of the stairway their passports and visas. She stamps them, hands them back and they are all allowed to bypass the regular passenger terminal.

Vladimir, Yuri, Serge and Aleks get into one limo and the rest of the men get into the other two. Then all three limos drive through the parking lot and enter the city street. The limos pull up to a hotel unloading zone where parking attendants are waiting. They all get out of the limos and walk toward the hotel entrance.

The men are now in a large elevator in the hotel. Vladimir pushes the up button and the elevator climbs to the ninth floor. The door opens and the men walk to room 911 and go inside. A bus boy comes down the hall and knocks on the 911 door. He has four bottles of wine and glasses on the cart he is pushing. One of the men opens the door, takes the cart from the bus boy, gives him a five dollar tip then shuts the door. The men then pour themselves wine.

"Vladimir, I understand you and your brother are here to find the woman who worked with Ivan Sakalov". Vladimir waves his hand in front of Serge.

"From now on Serge, speak English. All of us in this room speak English perfectly plus six other languages including Spanish and French. That's one of the reasons the men in here with Yuri and I have been chosen for this job . . . and yes, Yuri and I want to find that woman to see if she knows anything about what Sakalov did with the K Fifty Five information after he destroyed the computer".

CHAPTER 10

The three black limos that were at the Palm Springs hotel are now parked in front of the American-Russian Social Club in Los Angeles. Inside the club, men and women are drinking and dancing to loud music. The men who came in from Palm Springs are sitting at tables in a corner of the room. Vladimir and Yuri are with them and so is Serge. Scantily dressed young women are talking to them in Russian. The men are laughing and touching the women. John and Trishka are sitting at the bar watching the action at the tables. John gets up, walks past the bar and stands in the corner of the room. He takes out his cell phone and pretends to make a call. Instead, he takes pictures of the group of men that came in from Palm Springs. Then John goes back and sits down next to Trishka. Georgy Bondar, one of the Russian men who came in from Palm Springs is staring at John. Georgy gets up, goes over to Serge and takes him aside.

"What is it Georgy"?

"That man talking to the girl at the bar is FBI". Serge looks surprised.

"How do you know"?

"I'm positive. When I came to Los Angeles from Moscow to visit you last year, the Los Angeles District Attorney took me in and wanted to question me about the death of the man who used to own this building. I didn't have to say anything because I have diplomatic immunity. Remember"?

"Yes, Georgy, I remember" Georgy looks over at John.

"Well that man was in the District Attorney's office when I was brought in. I saw an FBI tag on his suit jacket".

Serge angrily looks over at John. Then he turns to Georgy.

"Georgy, I want you to follow him wherever he goes".

Serge goes over to the group of men that came in from Palm Springs and motions to them. They follow him upstairs to his office. They all walk in and Serge closes the door. Serge opens a suitcase and takes out Glock 27 pistols and gives each man one along with a box of bullets.

"Do not use those guns unless it is absolutely necessary. If you do use the gun, you all have diplomatic immunity, so the chances are you wouldn't be punished unless Russia waived your immunity, which could happen. So be very careful. Besides, I don't want any adverse publicity".

John and Jubas are in Jubas' office once again looking at Jubas television set. Jubas is at his DVD player.

"Rick, I want you to focus in on each man standing around the murder scene of the teachers on the DVD you showed me before".

Jubas stops the DVD player and focuses in on the first man in the group. It's Vladimir, but John doesn't recognize him because when John looks at the pictures on his cell phone he doesn't recognize Vladimir who now has long hair, a beard and no tattoos on his arms, while Vladimir who appears on the DVD that Jubas first showed John has short hair, is clean shaven and has tattoos on his arms, so he looks nothing at all like

82

Vladimir at the club. Therefore, John shakes his head "no". Jubas pushes a button on the DVD player and focuses in on the second man in the group. It's Yuri but John doesn't recognize him either because Yuri at the club has a shaved head a mustache, but no beard and tattoo free arms, while Yuri on the DVD has long hair, a large beard and his arms are covered with tattoos. So John shakes his head "no" again. Jubas pushes the button on the DVD player and focuses in on Georgy, the third face on the DVD. John looks at the picture on his cell phone he took at the club and shakes his head "yes". Jubas does the same close ups of the rest of the men standing around the murder scene and except for Vladimir and Yuri, John recognizes the rest of them as the men he took pictures of with his cell phone camera at the club.

"All those men were at the club, Rick except for the first two and I'm positive I've seen the third man you showed me on your DVD somewhere besides the club, but I can't remember where".

CHAPTER 11

John and his son Sam are heading out of the Marina Del Rey harbor on John's fishing boat. As John steers the boat through the harbor he remembers the happy time he had with Sam and Sara when they took the boat to Catalina and went on a bus tour of the island with all its wonders. John remembers the wild buffalo, foxes, mule deer and the beautiful birds as the bus took them around the island. He thought about how he missed looking at Sara's beautiful face as she pointed to the Arabian horse galloping around the arena at the old Wrigley Ranch. John reaches over and pats the top of Sam's head.

"I love you my son".

Sam hugs John.

"I love you too, daddy".

John points to Sam's tennis shoes.

"How do you like those shoes I got you?"

"They're great for my karate class. My old tennis shoes were too loose but these fit perfectly.

Thanks. I'll probably only wear them until you get me a new pair". They both laugh.

"How's your karate class going?"

"Watch this dad!"

Sam gives the post holding the boat's sail a wild side kick and the sail comes tumbling down. John grabs the sail.

"That was fantastic, Sam".

"It's called a side kick, dad. My teacher told me I'm one of the best in my class and that I'll probably have a black belt next year".

John pats Sam on the shoulder, then takes a pair of shoe laces out of his pocket and hands them to Sam.

"Here son, toss your old shoe laces and use these. They'll make your shoes even tighter on your feet".

Sam sits down on the boat deck, removes his old shoe laces and replaces them with the new ones.

The boat pulls up to the dock and John ties it to the rail. Then he and Sam walk to John's car. Georgy is sitting in his car and he takes pictures of John and Sam with his camera. John and Sam drive off and Georgy follows them.

John and Sam drive east on the 10 freeway to the 405. Then they get off at Sunset Boulevard and go east. Sam turns the radio on to a hip hop station. John frowns.

"God, Sam I hate that stuff.

Sam turns the radio to a classical music station and covers his ears. John laughs, and turns the sound higher. They both laugh. John turns left on Harper Avenue and pulls up in front of Angela's house. Sam gets out of the car and waves goodbye to John.

"Say hi to your aunt Angela for me", "Ok, dad".

The front door opens and Angela comes out. She waves at John. He waves back and throws her a kiss. Then he says to himself out loud.

"Thank you Angela you angel".

Georgy is watching all of what is going on from his car which is parked down the street. John drives off and Georgy follows him. John turns into the driveway of his house in Sherman Oaks. Georgy drives by the house slowly.

Later, John is sitting at the bar of the Russian club. Trishka is sitting next to him. They are talking and laughing. Serge comes up to John and taps him on the shoulder. John turns and looks at him. Serge speaks harsly.

"I don't like government agents in here". John is startled.

"You're FBI aren't you"?

John stares at Serge momentarily, then speaks in a friendly manner.

"I was, but they fired me because I didn't tell them I was half Russian when I signed their employment agreement. When they found out that my dad was Russian, the bastards fired me with no severance pay. I want nothing more to do with the FBI. I hate them".

Serge turns to Trishka.

"Let me see some identification".

Trishka takes out her wallet and hands Serge the driver's license that John gave her. Serge looks at the picture, then at her and gives her back her license. He motions his hand for her to leave. After Trishka leaves, Serge turns to John.

"Why should I trust you"? John replies in Russian.

"How about giving me a chance?"

Serge walks away and John leaves the club. He gets in his car and drives off. Georgy follows him.

Serge opens the door to his office at the club and he and Trishka walk in. Serge closes the door and starts fondling Trishka. She pulls away, leaves the office and slams the door behind her.

John comes out of his house the next morning, walks to his car, gets in and drives off. Luckily, Georgy is asleep in the driver's seat of his car so he's unable to follow John.

John parks his car behind a Starbucks coffee shop and walks in. His LAPD friend, Peter James is sitting at a table. He's wearing his police uniform. John goes to the counter and orders a cup of coffee, then sits down across from Peter at the table.

"Pete, they found out that I'm FBI and I told them I was fired because I never told the agency that I'm Russian. Serge, the owner of the club doesn't trust me and I need you to set him straight. If you could come to the club tonight I'll tell Serge that I know you're a cop and ask you to leave and it may get a little rough".

"We've got to bring those assholes down John".

"When you come in I'll walk up to where Serge is and stand next to him. He usually comes down to the bar about eight o'clock".

"Ok John, see you tonight".

John is sitting at the bar in the club alone. Serge is at a table in the corner talking to Vladimir and Yuri. Peter James comes in the front door. He's dressed in street clothes. John gets up and walks over to the table where Serge is and stands there. Peter sees where John is and begins a conversation with a young lady on the dance floor right near the table where Serge is sitting. John goes up to Peter and taps him on the shoulder. Then

John raises his voice so Serge can hear him above the noise of the crowd.

"We don't want police in here".

"I'm not a cop".

"That's bullshit! I know who you are, Peter James from the North Hollywood Police Station". John yells.

"Now get out!"

Peter gives John a nasty look and throws his drink on the floor. Then he storms out the front door. John goes back to the bar and motions to the bartender. Serge watches as the bartender comes over to John. "I'll have a Bud Light".

The bartender brings the beer to John. John reaches in his pocket and takes out some money. Serge walks over and whispers in the bartender's ear, who then refuses to take any money from John. John smiles and waves to Serge.

John and Trishka are driving down Ventura Boulevard in Studio City. John turns right on Carpenter Avenue, then turns right on Laurelwood Drive and stops in front of a nice looking multiple unit apartment building.

"Laurelwood Drive is a safe street, Trish. Let's check this place out".

John and Trishka are inside a one bedroom furnished apartment with the manager, Ronald Fisk.

"Well, how do you like it?"

"It's perfect, mister Fisk. Are you ok with Nancy?"

Trishka looks happy.

"I love it John". Fisk hands John the lease agreement. John looks it over.

"A thousand a month?"

"Yep". John points to Trishka.

"Nancy is going to be living here, but I'll be paying the rent".

Fisk looks Trishka up and down. She smiles at him, he smiles back.

"May I see some identification Ms Stenson?" She takes out her driver's license and shows it to Fisk.

"So you're single?"

"Yes".

John signs and initials the lease and hands it to Fisk who signs it.

"I'll pay you the entire amount now."

"Ok. It's three thousand dollars. First month, last month and one month's security deposit".

John takes out his checkbook, writes numbers on it, signs it and hands it to Fisk, who looks at it then shakes his head up and down.

"I'll get you a set of keys".

The next evening Trishka is sitting on the couch in the living room of her apartment, reading a book. Her cell phone rings and she picks it up and listens for awhile. Then she shakes her head and says.

"Yes John, I left the club early. I just had to get away from there." She listens, then says.

"Chinese is fine, but get me some Wonton soup, ok?"

She smiles and says.

"I'll leave the door unlocked for you". Trishka closes her cell phone and walks around the dining area lighting candles. Then she takes a bottle of wine from the refrigerator and puts it on the dining room table along with glasses, dishes, silverware and napkins.

Later, John comes in carrying bags of Chinese food. They both fill their plates and John pours the wine and they sit down to eat. Suddenly, extremely loud voices, music and laughter can be heard coming through the dining room wall.

"What the hell is that?"

"It's from the apartment next door, John. Just like last night. I'll call the manager because I can't stand the noise".

Fisk comes down the hall with two large men and he knocks on Trishka's door. She opens it. The noise from her neighbor is deafening.

"I'll take care of this for you Nancy".

Fisk goes next door and bangs on the door. The door opens and Trishka's neighbor confronts Fisk with very loud music in the background. There are various other people, men and women in the apartment dancing around.

"I told you Samansky, no more noise!"

Fisk turns to one of the men with him and speaks to him in Russian.

"Go in there and get me the CD machine".

Samansky, the neighbor is furious and he says in Russian.

"Hey, what the fuck do you think you're doing?"

The music stops and Fisk's man comes out with the CD machine. Fisk motions to the man, who throws the machine onto the floor then crushes it under his shoe. Fisk looks at the neighbor and says in Russian.

"Next time that will be your head. Now get back in your apartment and tell your friends to shut the fuck up!"

Samansky looks at Fisk, then at Fisk's two men and backs into his apartment then shuts the door. Fisk goes back to John and Trishka

"You won't have any more trouble with him or his friends. They're all in this country illegally and they'll keep their mouths shut."

Later, John and Trishka are cleaning up her apartment. John comes over and starts to unbutton her blouse. She takes it off, then takes off her pants. She's standing there in her bra and panties. John carries her to the bedroom and gently puts her down on the bed. He gets on top of her. But the back of her head where she was injected seems to bother her, so she slowly pulls herself out from under John and says. "I like being on top".

She gets on top of John, kisses him then takes off her bra and panties. He strokes her naked shoulders. They make love. Afterwards, Trishka is lying next to John under the covers. John turns to Trishka.

"Trish, you should see a doctor about those migraines". She looks at him and says. "I'll be ok".

She turns away and closes her eyes. John stares at her back. Trishka opens her eyes and has a sad look on her face. John is now facing the other way and can't see her face. Trishka says to John in Russian. "I feel so close to you". John answers in Russian. "I think I'm falling in love with you Trishka".

She kisses him, then turns on her side away from him and softly cries. "Good night John".

John turns over and looks into her eyes. Then strokes her face. "Good night my beautiful one".

Morning light is filtering in through the window. John is getting dressed. Trishka wakes up and touches John's hand. "Should I make you breakfast?"

"No, Trish. I have work to do this morning. Last night was fantastic". "Yes it was".

John walks out of Trishka's apartment, gets in his car and drives to his house in Sherman Oaks. Georgy is sitting in the driver's seat of his car a few houses down from John's house. John pulls his car into the driveway, goes into the house, comes out a few minutes later, gets into his car and drives away. Georgy follows him.

Georgy is a few car lengths behind John's car as John pulls up to the Federal Building and parks in a no parking zone. Sidney Manning, the computer genius comes out the front door, walks to John's car and gets in. Georgy picks up his cell phone and dials.

"He's at the Federal Building. I think there is something important going on. Sidney Manning the computer expert you showed me a picture of and told me about, just got into Mason's car with him".

Serge is on the phone in his office in the Russian club. Vladimir and Yuri are in the office with him.

"Georgy, Sidney Manning is going to be interviewed on Channel 3 about computers at eight o'clock tonight. Mason is coming over to have drinks with me and I want you to be here."

CHAPTER 12

Serge puts down the cell phone and looks and Vladimir and Yuri.

"I think Mason is a spy for the FBI and he's lied to us. I'll keep playing his game so we can see what he's really up to. We know where his son lives. I'll let you know if and when to act. In the meantime Vladimir, go to the Longshoremen's Union meeting tomorrow and meet with Afonos Mirski. He owes me a gambling debt and I'm certain he'll help us. You know how important it is for us to get the Solntsevos involved in the Longshoremen's Union. Here's a picture of Afonos. Give him my regards".

Serge gives Vladimir the picture of a gruff looking man. That evening Serge, John and Georgy are having drinks in Serge's office at the Russian club. Serge turns the television on to Channel 3. The newscaster is interviewing Sidney Manning. Manning is talking about how computers are going to totally change the world in the future. All three men are watching the program. Serge turns to John.

"He really knows about computers doesn't he"?

John fills his glass with beer.

"I've heard of Sidney Manning. The man seems brilliant".

Serge's facial expression changes as he turns away from John and looks at Georgy.

The next morning John is making himself breakfast. His cell phone rings and he clicks it on.

"Hello Rick. The car dealer's sending someone to pick up my car. It needs servicing. He's bringing me a rental so I'll be at your office in about an hour".

Just then, John's doorbell rings and he opens the door. It's the driver from the dealership. John looks at his watch and smiles.

"You're right on time".

The driver hands John keys for the rental. John hands the driver his keys and the man turns around and waves.

"Your car should be ready tomorrow about noon sir".

The driver gets in John's car which is parked in the driveway, backs out and drives off. Georgy, who's parked almost a block away starts his car and follows John's car. In the meantime, John leaves the house, gets into the rental car and drives off in the opposite direction.

John parks the rental car down the street from the FBI Building, gets out and puts his credit card in the meter. Then he walks across the street and goes into the building. Jubas is sitting behind his desk when John walks in.

"John, the big boys want you to keep records of all the money you spend taking care of Trishka, as well as all other monies you charge on the FBI credit card. But here's the good news. For working under cover, you'll be getting a big chunk of change courtesy of President Farley".

Jubas hands John some paperwork.

"Fill in these forms and I'll get them to the proper people. I'm going up to Bakersfield in about a half hour to look at some horse property. My wife loves horses. You want to join us?"

John remembers when his father used to take him horseback riding in Burbank almost every weekend when he was growing up. He became so proficient at riding that he entered an equestrian contest which was to be held in Hidden Hills, but his father had a heart attack the day before the contest so John spent the entire weekend at the hospital with his mother and missed the contest. John turns to Jubas.

"I love horses too, Rick".

Jubas hands John a copy of the real estate listing.

"We shouldn't be seen driving together so meet us at the ranch if you don't mind the drive".

"Not at all Rick".

John, Jubas, Jubas' wife Marilyn and the real estate broker are walking around the stable area at the ranch. Horses are looking out of their stalls at them. Jubas turns to his wife.

"What do you think, honey".

"Oh Rick. I love it!"

John pats a horse on the nose.

"So do I".

John asks the broker.

"How many acres does it have?"

"About nineteen and a half."

"How come it's so cheap?"

"Because the owner lost his construction business and had to declare bankruptcy. He paid almost three and a half million for the place four years ago. It's really a good deal at a million two hundred thousand. But you'll need six hundred thousand for the down payment".

John, Jubas and Marilyn are together in the living room and the broker is outside getting into his car. Jubas looks at the blueprints.

"The main house is over forty two hundred square feet and the guest house is over two thousand square feet."

Jubas looks at Marilyn. She's overjoyed.

"I really love this place Rick. We should buy it. I've got to go to the bathroom".

Jubas points to an open door in the hall. Marilyn goes in to the bathroom and shuts the door. John looks at Jubas.

"You can use the chunk of money I'm getting from President Farley plus what I've got in my savings account for the down payment".

"Ok John, but I want you on title with us."

They shake hands and Marilyn comes out of the bathroom.

"Honey, John said he'll make the down payment, but I want him to own this ranch with us. Are you ok with that?"

Marilyn smiles and hugs John.

"Of course it's ok with me".

Jubas picks up his briefcase and goes to the front door.

"Let's meet the broker at his office and make this official. John, you can follow us in your car".

Jubas and Marilyn walk to their car and John walks to his rental car. Jubas drives away and John follows.

Jubas, John and Marilyn are sitting at a conference table in the real estate broker's office. The broker comes in holding a folder. He opens it and spreads the papers on the table.

"The lender accepted your offer".

Jubas stands up and shakes the broker's hand.

"That's great! Just make sure that mister Mason is one of the owners of the ranch along with my wife and me".

"I certainly will mister Jubas. Now if you three will sign these documents, I'll messenger them to the lender and in a couple of weeks the ranch will be yours".

The broker begins gathering up the paperwork. Jubas, Marilyn and John stand in a circle holding hands.

CHAPTER 13

Serge and Georgy are standing next to Serge's desk in his office at the Russian club. Serge stares at Georgy and raises his voice.

"What do you mean you noticed Mason wasn't driving his car?" Georgy looks worried.

"I followed his car, but when it stopped for a red light I saw there was someone else driving. I don't know what happened". "So you lost Mason!" "I'm sorry, I didn't know". Serge is extremely angry now. He points to the door and raises his voice. "Go downstairs to the bar and tell Nancy to come up here!" Georgy leaves the room with a frightened look on his face. He walks up to Trishka who is sitting at the bar having a glass of wine. "Serge wants to see you now."

Trishka gets up still holding her wine glass and follows Georgy upstairs. Georgy leaves her in front of Serge's office and walks away. She knocks on the door.

"Who's there?" "It's Nancy".

The door opens and Serge motions with his hand to come in. "You wanted to see me?"

"Yes, I haven't been paid for working last night". "You only worked part time". "Then pay me half".

"If you don't work the entire evening, you get nothing!" Trishka is very upset. "That's not fair Serge".

"It's mister Koszmakoff to you. Now show me some ID", She puts her wine glass down on a coffee table and shows Serge her driver's license. Serge looks at the license, then at Trishka. She holds out her hand.

"Now pay me what you owe me!"

"Just get out of here and don't ever leave early again without my permission!"

CHAPTER 14

She quickly walks out. Serge picks up his cell phone.

"Come up to my office".

Yuri is going up the stairs to Serge's office and he almost runs into Trishka who is running down the stairs. He goes to the office, opens the door and Serge is on his cell phone. He finishes his call when Yuri comes in. Serge picks up Trishka's wine glass which he has wrapped in a paper towel. He hands the glass to Yuri.

"I don't usually ask the women who work here for their identification, but I had an argument with Nancy and I detected a Russian accent. Her fingerprints are on this wine glass. Yuri, take this glass to Dimitri Potemkin at the Russian Embassy. He's a friend and he's going to have her fingerprints checked. I just spoke to Dimitri. He's there waiting for you".

Yuri takes the glass, leaves the office and shuts the door behind him.

Dimitri Potemkin is on the telephone in his office at the Russian Embassy. Yuri is standing next to him.

"Serge, I sent the fingerprints through. We can find no record of that girl in the United States".

"What about the Department of Motor Vehicles?" "Nothing there either Serge".

Serge is sitting behind his desk at the Russian club. He is on his cell phone.

"Can you have her fingerprints checked in Russia, Dimitri?" Dimitri turns to Yuri.

"You say your contact in Moscow can analyze her fingerprints?" "Yes, Dimitri. I went to college with Aleksei. He's an expert at finding out if a person has a history in Russia by checking their fingerprints. Let me use your telephone and I will call him". Dimitri picks up his phone and hands it to Yuri, who dials Aleksei's number. He speaks Russian to Aleksei.

"Aleksei it's Yuri Mikhail". Aleksei speaks Russian to Yuri. "I know . . . . how are you?"

"I'm fine. Listen, I need a favor. I have a set of fingerprints I can fax you and I'd like to know if you could check this person's history in Russia for me".

"No Aleksei I only have a fax copy of her prints". Yuri shakes his head.

"Yes I realize that a fax copy is not as good as the original my friend, but could you please see if you can do me this favor?" "Alright. What is your fax number".

Yuri writes down the numbers and hands the paper to Dimitri. "Thank you Aleksei. I'll have Dimitri fax you her prints. Goodbye" Dimitri has the paper he used to check out Trishka's fingerprints. He puts it in the fax machine and punches in the numbers Yuri gave him. The paper goes through.

Serge and Yuri are in Serge's office at the Russian club. The bartender comes in and gives them each a bottle of beer. They start drinking and Serge's phone rings. He picks it up.

"Hello . . . oh yes Aleksei, Yuri's right here". Serge hands Yuri the phone.

"Hello Aleksei,. Have you been able to check those fingerprints out? Ok, give me a minute".

Yuri grabs a pencil and paper, then gets back on the phone. "Yes, ok".

Yuri is on the phone with Aleksei while writing on the paper. "She was in the army, uh huh . . . and she was Ivan Sakalov's secretary. Ok".

Serge looks amazed. Yuri continues writing.

"What is her name?"

Yuri writes on the paper.

"And she was born in Kiev. Thank you Aleksei. I owe you".

Yuri hangs up the phone. Looks over at Serge who is totally outraged.

"When is Vladimir coming back from his meeting with the union members, Serge?"

Serge just stares at the wall, then he turns to Yuri.

"Later tonight".

Yuri looks at the paper he wrote on while he was on the phone with Aleksei.

"Her name is Trishka Perova and I'm sure she's working with that bastard FBI agent John Mason. I'm going to find her now and hold her until I see what Vladimir wants to do with her."

Serge clicks on his cell phone.

"Georgy, this is Serge. Did you follow that woman who calls herself Nancy Stenson?"

Georgy is in his car across the street from the apartment building where Trishka lives. He's on his cell phone with Serge.

"She just got out of her car in front of her apartment in Studio City".

Serge is staring at Yuri while he's talking to Georgy.

"Ok, good. Now leave her place, go back to Mason's house and see if you can track him down".

He clicks his cell phone off, writes something on a piece of paper and says to Yuri.

"She went to her apartment".

He hands the piece of paper to Yuri.

"Here is her address. Tell her I gave you some money for her. That way she'll let you in".

Yuri is driving. He turns right on Laurelwood from Carpenter and stops in front of the apartment house where Trishka lives. He gets out of his car, walks up the brick entryway and sees Ronald Fisk the manager on his knees planting flowers in the garden. Fisk is on his cell phone speaking Russian.

"I need ten bags of fertilizer delivered tomorrow". Fisk listens on is phone. Then says in Russian.

"Thank you very much".

Fisk closes the phone and looks up at Yuri.

"Can I help you?" Yuri speaks to Fisk in Russian.

"Yes, I'm looking for Nancy Stenson's apartment". Fisk points up to the second floor.

"Number 217".

"Thanks".

Trishka is in her apartment on the couch in the living room watching television. Knock on the door. She gets up and walks to the door.

"Who's there?"

"It's Yuri from the club. Serge gave me some money for you".

Trishka opens the door. Yuri barges in. Raises his voice.

"Your name isn't Nancy Stenson, it's Trishka Perova!"

Yuri shows Trishka her original Russian passport. She sees herself with blond hair and blue eyes. She is startled and just stares at Yuri. Yuri, asks her in Russian.

"Where is Mason?"

"I don't know".

Yuri takes out his pistol which has a silencer attached. He points it at Trishka's chest.

"You're coming with me".

He touches the back of her head.

"Vladimir wants to see what the doctor put in there".

Trishka stands her ground. Yuri comes closer and has his finger on the trigger. Suddenly Trishka ducks and smashes her body into Yuri. He falls back.

She grabs the pistol from his hand, points it at his head the pulls the trigger. The bullet hits Yuri right between the eyes and he goes down in a pool of blood. Trishka runs to her cell phone and dials.

John has just left the off ramp of the 405 freeway and is going east on the 101 freeway. He's just minutes away from Trishka's apartment.

His cell phone rings. He clicks it on. It's Trishka and she's totally crazed.

"John, it's Trishka. Please come to my apartment now. I just shot Yuri!"

John's eyes open wide, his hand shakes as he holds the cell phone to his ear.

"I'm almost there!"

Trishka clicks her cell phone off and looks down at Yuri who's face is covered with blood and his dead eyes are open.

John pulls his car up in front of the apartment building where Trishka is, gets out of the car and walks by Fisk who's still on his knees planting flowers. He waves to John and John waves back. Then John goes inside, and knocks on Trishka's door.

"It's John".

She's crying hysterically as she opens the door and wraps her arms around John. He sees Yuri dead on the floor. John quickly shuts the door.

"What the hell happened?" Trishka tries to speak but she's sobbing so loudly that she can't say anything. John looks into her eyes.

"Trish . . . tell me!" Trishka looks up at John and speaks in a broken high pitched voice.

"Yuri pointed a gun at me and was going to take me with him. I was able to get the gun away and I shot him".

John gets on his knees and wipes the blood away from Yuri's face.

"Jesus Christ! That's Yuri? He looks like a different person. Vladimir must have changed the way he used to look too. That's why I didn't recognize either of them!"

John looks around the room and sees the blood on the wall and floor. He turns to Trishka.

"We've got to get his body out of here!"

Fisk is still planting flowers when John comes out of the apartment house like nothing's wrong. He smiles at Fisk who waves back. John gets in the rental car and drives to the garage in back of the apartment building and parks the car right next to the garage door. John walks back around the building and looks at Fisk.

"I forgot something".

Fisk shakes his head and smiles. John goes back to Trishka's apartment. He and Trishka wipe the blood stains from the floor and wall with towels. They wash the towels and hang them up. John finds the empty brass shell casing from the bullet that Trishka shot at Yuri. He puts the shell casing and Yuri's gun in his pocket. Then he and Trishka wrap Yuri in large blankets. John makes certain no one is in the hallway and he and Trishka drag Yuri's body which is covered with blankets down the hall to the emergency exit. The exit door is alarmed so John deactivates the alarm, opens the door and they drag Yuri's body down the stairs and into the garage. John opens the car trunk and they lift Yuri's body, put it in the trunk and John closes the lid. Trishka grabs John's hand.

"John, I must tell you what happened to me in Russia". John and Trishka drive up to John's boat. John parks the car next to the boat. It's dark and there's no one in sight. Trishka puts her arms around John.

"So Ivan Sakalov had the doctor inject a chip from the K Fifty Five computer into the back of your head?"

"Yes he did. That's why my head hurts when it's touched. I don' think Ivan told anyone but me that it contained the contents of the red box from the Russian K Fifty Five computer. He thought he could make a fortune if he sold me to the Russian mafia, but before he had a chance to do that, I escaped from Russia and Ivan was killed. He did tell me that I would die a horrible death if someone tried to take the chip out. Vladimir must know that something important was injected into my head. Yuri said Vladimir was going to find out what was injected into me". Trishka starts sobbing and John strokes her arms. "I'm never going to let anything bad happen to you Trishka. That's a promise from my heart. Now let's get rid of Yuri's body".

John gets out of the car after making sure nobody's anywhere near them. The entire place is deserted because it's so late at night. He goes back to the car and he and Trishka unload Yuri's body and carry it to John's boat. John is at the helm and Trishka is next to him. The lights from the coastline are barely visible because they are out in the ocean many miles from the California coast. John shuts down the engine. "I think we've gone far enough".

He and Trishka drag Yuri's body to the side of the boat, unroll the blankets and let the body fall into the ocean. John tosses the brass shell casing over the side, but keeps Yuri's pistol. Then John starts the engine, turns the boat around and heads back. John points to where they just were. "The sharks will probably destroy his body". The next morning Vladimir and two of the Russian men that came with him from Palm Springs pull up in front of the apartment building where Trishka lives. They get out of the car, walk to the building and go inside. Vladimir knocks on manager Fisk's door. Fisk opens the door. "Can I help you?"

"We work with Nancy Stenson, but she's not answering her phone. Have you seen her?"

"No, but yesterday afternoon a man asked me for her apartment number and went inside. He spoke Russian." Vladimir says in Russian "Was his head shaved?" Fisk shakes his head "yes". Vladimir says. "I'm sure that was my brother".

Nancy works with us at the American-Russian club downtown, but she didn't come to work last night". Then Fisk says.

"The man who rented the apartment also came to see her a short time after your brother came". Vladimir asks.

"Was it John Mason?"

"Yes. I had the floodlights on outside and I was working on the yard all night, but I didn't see them leave. If they're not inside, they must have used the emergency exit, but the door is alarmed. They must have turned off the alarm. But why?"

Vladimir and Serge are sitting on the couch in Serge's upstairs office at the Russian club having drinks.

Vladimir puts his drink down.

"I've been calling Yuri all day and he doesn't answer his phone". Then Serge says.

"I must have called him fifty times today and he didn't answer me either".

Vladimir looks very upset.

"No one has seen or heard from that lying bitch Trishka Perova or Mason. Something's wrong, very wrong".

Serge looks at his wrist watch.

"For now, Vladimir we both need rest. It's two thirty five in the morning".

Vladimir goes to the door

"Goodnight Serge".

An exhausted looking Vladimir and the other Russian men he brought from Palm Springs are sitting at the dining room table having breakfast in Vladimir's rented house in Hollywood. The news is being broadcast on a giant flat screen television set hanging on a wall above them. Vladimir puts his hands behind his head.

"Nobody has heard from my brother in over four days. I'm so worried I can't sleep".

Suddenly the newscaster goes to "breaking news".

"The LAPD has advised that they have identified the man's body that the Coast Guard found yesterday floating in the ocean with a gunshot to the head. DNA tests confirmed that the man is Yuri Mikhail, a Russian diplomatic attache".

CHAPTER 15

Vladimir's body begins to shake. He stands up and cries out. Then his cell phone rings. He doesn't pay attention at first, then he looks at the phone's screen. It's Serge who's calling. He clicks it on. "Did you see the news about your brother"?

"I know it was Mason and Trishka who killed him. They're going to die!"

"Georgy followed Mason and his son to the Marina the other day. Mason's got a small yacht. They probably took Yuri's body on the boat then threw it in the ocean. Georgy knows where Mason's son lives, Vladimir". "Get me the address now Serge!"

Vladimir and his men are in a car parked a few houses down from Angela's house. A school bus goes past them but doesn't stop. A short time later, Angela pulls into the driveway. She and Sam get out of her car and walk towards the house. Vladimir and his men look around to make sure no one is watching. When the coast is clear, they get out of the car and follow Angela and

Sam. Vladimir grabs Angela and one of his men grabs Sam.

Angela screams and Vladimir slams his giant hand around her mouth. The man holding Sam knocks him out. Vladimir takes Angela's keys from her, opens the front door and shoves her into the house.

"Where is John Mason?"

Angela is totally frightened and answers in a shaky voice.

"I don't know".

"I said where is John Mason!?"

"I . . . I don't know".

Vladimir snaps his finger at one of his men who takes out a pocket knife, opens it and hands it to Vladimir who cuts Angela's neck wide open. As blood begins to gush out, Sam wakes up and when he sees what Vladimir has done to his aunt he begins to scream and cry. Vladimir gives the man holding Sam a signal and the man knocks Sam out again. Vladimir and his men wait until a man walking his dog past the house is out of sight, then they walk to the car. Sam is still unconscious and is carried to the car by one of the men and put in the back seat next to Vladimir. The others get in the car and they drive off.

Serge is on a pay phone in a Von's market parking lot.

"Is this the Los Angeles FBI office? Ok, then tell whoever knows John Mason the we're holding his son. Do you have a cell phone number for mister Mason?"

Someone speaks to Serge on the other end.

"I'm telling you, if you don't give me Mason's number right now, his son will die!"

There's silence on the phone for a short time, then a voice can be heard. Serge takes out a pen and writes a number on his hand. Then he hangs up the pay phone after wiping off his fingerprints.

Serge, and Anton and Ilya, two of the Palm Springs Russians have Georgy on Serge's office floor at the club. Anton has his hands around Georgy's neck. Serge brings his face up to Georgy's face.

"You lost Mason. Now you must pay".

Serge motions to Anton who twists Georgy's neck, breaking it. Then Serge looks at Anton.

"Anton, take Ilya with you and bury Georgy in the desert where no one will find the body"

Serge hands Anton a map.

"I've marked the general area where you can bury him. It's in Death Valley. Take the Buick with the GPS".

Ilya and Anton drag Georgy's body out of the room. Serge writes on a piece of paper and hands it to Fedor, another Russian man he brought in from Palm Springs.

"That's Mason's home address Fedor. Get inside his house and wait. He may come back there for clothes or something. If he does, you know what to do. If Trishka is with him kill her too, but do not damage her head in any way. Do you understand?"

Fedor shakes his head "yes".

Jubas opens the front door to his house and lets John and Trishka in. Jubas' wife Marilyn comes into the living room with a tray of food, puts it on a table then leaves the room. John looks scared and is trembling.

"What happened, John?"

"Someone called the FBI office and said my son's been kidnapped. The police are at Angela's house now. She's been murdered!" Jubas' jaw drops.

"A doctored voice called me from a pay phone and said the people he works with would trade Sam for Trishka".

Serge and Vladimir are in Serge's office at the social club.

"Don't worry Vladimir. I'll have my men take John's son to my old warehouse in Sylmar. You go to the county coroner's department and examine the body to make sure it's Yuri".

Vladimir is staring at the floor. Serge gives him a map and a card.

"Use this map to find the county coroner's department. When you get there ask for Stephen Billings. Tell him Serge from the Russian Embassy asked you to check the body to make certain it's Yuri Mikhail. Just show him the official Russian Embassy card I gave you".

Trishka, Jubas and John are upstairs in Jubas' master bedroom. John takes out a device that looks like a tiny cell phone and clicks it on. It beeps a few times then stops. John opens it and takes out two small batteries. He turns to Jubas.

"The batteries are dead Rick. Do you have two triple A's?" Jubas shakes his head yes, then goes out of the room. A few minutes later he comes back upstairs with two triple A batteries and gives them to John. John puts them in the device and it begins beeping. Jubas points to the device.

"What's that?"

"It's a tracer and it works like a GPS. It will find the electronic bug in Sam's shoelaces so I'll be able to trace the location where they're hiding him". Jubas looks at John.

CHAPTER 16

"How do you know he's wearing the shoes with the traceable laces?"

"Sam only wears the shoes I gave him".

John grabs Jubas by the arm and yells.

"Come on . . . . let's go!"

John and Jubas are speeding north on the 5 freeway. John is looking at the tracer. He points to the off ramp.

"Turn off at Osborne".

Jubas slows down and turns off and begins driving east. After a few minutes, John raises his hand.

"Ok, it says to go a couple hundred feet and we'll be there".

Jubas slows down to a crawl. Suddenly, a light on the tracer turns green.

"We're here".

Jubas stops the car in front of a large deserted unlit warehouse. John points to it.

"They've got Sam in there".

John and Jubas make sure their guns are ready to fire. They get out of the car and silently make their way around a broken fence to the side of the building. John peers inside a closed window and whispers to Jubas.

"They have Sam tied up in a chair. It's dark inside but somebody's got a flashlight shining on him".

Jubas whispers back.

"Yeah. I see Sam and two men standing next to him".

One of the men asks Sam something but Sam doesn't answer, so the man picks up a large piece of wood from the floor and slams it against Sam's forehead. John whispers.

"Son of a bitch. Let's go around the back. That way we might be able to get the drop on those bastards".

John and Jubas very slowly and silently go around the building to the back. They find a door that's almost completely off its hinges. John delicately pulls at the door and it opens just enough to let them sneak inside and crawl towards Sam and the men. When they are close, they draw their pistols. John stands up and yells at the men in Russian.

"Down on the floor!"

Serge and Fedor are in Serge's home office. Serge is trying to call on his cell phone.

"They're not answering. Go to the warehouse and see what's wrong".

Serge hands Fedor a map.

"It's about a ten minute drive from here Fedor".

The men at the warehouse see John and Jubas' pistols pointing at them. One of the men immediately drops to the floor. The second man raises his pistol and fires at John, but misses. John shoots him in the head and the man flies backward and slams into a steel stud. Sam yells.

"Dad look out!"

The other man on the floor goes for his gun. Jubas fires and hits the man in the side of the head, killing him. John rushes over to Sam, unties him and wipes the blood from his forehead. Sam is crying and hugs John.

Fedor pulls up behind a truck that's parked in front of a building next to the abandoned warehouse. He opens the car door to get out, but before he does he sees John, Jubas and Sam run out from the side of the warehouse, get into John's car and drive off. Fedor starts his car and follows them. He opens his cell phone.

"Serge, Mason and another man have taken the boy from the warehouse and they are driving away. I'm following them now".

John looks in his rear view mirror.

"I've seen that car that's behind us before".

John floors the accelerator and the car speeds down the road. He looks in the rear view mirror and the car that was following them has disappeared.

"I guess I was mistaken".

John pulls up in front of Jubas' house in Burbank. John, Jubas and Sam get out and hurry to the front door. Jubas knocks on the door and Marilyn opens it. They all hurry inside and she shuts the door.

Fedor pulls up behind John's car. He pulls a hoodie over his head, picks up his cell phone and dials.

"They've stopped at a house. 120 Eaton Street, Burbank".

Serge's on his cell phone.

Serge hands Vladimir his cell phone and says.

"It's Fedor".

Sam is bleeding from his forehead. John is holding a paper towel against the wound.

"Rick, I need some alcohol and bandages."

"Upstairs under the master bathroom sink. I'll get the stuff for you".

"It's ok Rick, I'll take Sam up there aid fix him up".

John carries Sam upstair.

Jubas happens to look out the window and sees Fedor sitting in his car in front of the house. Fedor is staring at him from under his hoodie. Jubas points to the car and says to Marilyn.

"I think that's the car that was following us from the warehouse".

Jubas' demeanor changes. He really appears nervous. He grabs his gun, motions to Marilyn and they go out the back door then head toward the street through the garden at the side of the house which lets them get close to Fedor's car without him being able to see them.

Fedor is still staring at Jubas window. He's on his cell phone with Vladimir. He doesn't see Jubas and Marilyn when they walk around the side of his car especially because his hoodie is blocking his side vision.

Jubas pounds on the car's side window. Fedor yells into the phone.

"They're banging on my car window!" Vladimir says.

"Open your window and see what they want".

Jubas yells at Fedor.

"Who sent you!"

Fedor's mouth drops open and he points his Glock at Jubas and fires through the window hitting Jubas in the chest, then he shoots Marilyn in the head. Fedor speeds away in his car when he sees John come running out of the house.

John goes to Jubas and Marilyn who are lying on the ground. A neighbor who was mowing his lawn comes running over. John drops to his knees and holds Jubas' face.

"Oh my God . . . they're both dead!"

The neighbor holds his chest then sits down, as John yells.

"Sam . . . Trishka, get out here now!"

Sam appears with a bandaged forehead. Trishka is right beside him. They look down in horror at the dead bodies. John, Sam and Trishka get into John's car. John floors it and flies up the street trying to catch Fedor.

Fedor is speeding down a side street and yelling into his cell phone.

"I shot the man who was with Mason and the woman who was with the man. Now Mason's after me!"

Serge is yelling into his cell phone too.

"The woman you shot better not have been Trishka Perova" Fedor looks at his phone, then answers.

"No. You showed me Perova's picture. The woman I shot was fat and had short red hair".

Serge looks relieved.

"I want you to get away from Mason. Do you understand?"

Fedor puts his cell phone down and is able to back his car behind a truck in someone's driveway. Suddenly, John's car speeds by the driveway. Fedor wait's a few minutes, then pulls out of the driveway and takes off in the opposite direction.

Sam is in the back seat with Trishka. He puts his head in her lap and cries. Trishka strokes his head.

Serge and Vladimir are sitting on the living room sofa in Serge's house. Serge gets up and starts walking around then he turns to Vladimir.

"I checked with a real estate broker I know. The house that Fedor saw them go into is owned by the FBI and it's rented to Rick and Marilyn Jubas. Then I called my friend at the Russian Embassy. He told me that Jubas was an FBI agent and said Jubas wife was fat, with short red hair. He told me both of them were killed today". Suddenly there is a loud banging at Serge's front door. Vladimir goes to a side window to see who it is.

"It's Fedor".

Vladimir opens the door and Fedor comes in totally shaking and wild eyed. Serge grabs Fedor by the arm and tosses him onto the couch.

"When he knocked on the car window why didn't you just speak to him?"

"Because he was yelling at me and I was frightened".

Vladimir takes out a large pocket knife and opens it. Sunlight shines on the blade as he walks over to Fedor and grabs him by the shirt.

"Are you frightened now asshole?"

Vladimir looks over at Serge who gives him a hand signal. Vladimir slices Fedor's neck from one side to the other and lets his dead body fall to the floor. Serge looks down at Fedor and spits on him.

"I'll have Ilya and Anton take his body to the desert and bury it next to Georgy. In the meantime, let's clean up the mess". Vladimir turns to Serge.

"I went to the Longshoremen's meeting yesterday like you told me to do. When the speakers finished I asked to see Afonos Mirski. One of the speakers told me that Mirski had been arrested that morning for drug trafficking. The secretary told me that Georgy met with Mirski the other day and that Georgy was upset when he left". Serge looks startled.

"What!?" Vladimir looks right at Serge.

"You mean you didn't send Georgy there?"

"No. The son of a bitch went there behind my back". Vladimir hits his fist on his other hand.

"Georgy must have turned Mirski in because he wouldn't let Georgy become part of the drug smuggling racket. I'll bet that's why Georgy was upset".

Serge stomps his foot on the floor.

"Mirski was my inside man there! Well at least we took care of the asshole Georgy".

"Do you know anyone else there that I can get information from?"

"No I don't, Vladimir".

"What should I tell my Solntsevos contacts in Moscow?"

Serge hesitates briefly.

"Tell them we need a little more time".

Vladimir looks worried.

"I'll tell them, but we don't want to mess with the Solntsevos if we want to see another summer. Don't forget Serge, they sent me here to infiltrate the Longshoremen's Union and they won't take no for an answer".

"I'll keep searching for Trishka Perova. When I find her I'll find out what she knows about the Russian K Fifty Five computer and what was injected into her skull. Maybe we'll have some answers that will help us satisfy the Solntsevos".

CHAPTER 17

John, Sam and Trishka are in a waiting room at FBI headquarters on the seventeenth floor of the Federal Building in West L.A. They stand up when FBI agent David Williams comes in.

"Your room is ready, folks".

They follow Williams down the hall to room 1709 and go inside.

It's early in the morning and Serge is pacing in his living room. The front door opens and two Russian men dressed in Department of Water and Power uniforms come in. Serge looks them over.

"Have they finished painting the truck yet?"

"In about one hour Serge. The truck looks exactly like a Los Angeles DWP repair truck. It's six years old has red lines going up the back of the tailgate with DWP seals on the outside of the front doors. I also installed the license plates you gave me".

"That's good, Desya. Now you and Evgeni take the truck and go to the Federal Building at 11000 Wilshire Boulevard just east of Sepulveda.

and remember, only speak English". Serge is holding a map and a small camera.

"This is a map of the area and a special camera that will take close up pictures. The FBI office is on the seventeenth floor of the building and there is a very large power pole just across the street from the building. I had one of my men cut off the power to the pole last night. While you and Evgeni are up on the pole, take pictures of anyone who looks like Mason or Trishka Perova and call me immediately if you see anyone who looks like either of them". Desya takes the map and camera.

Vladimir, Ilva and Anton come downstairs from the second floor.

Vladimir is wearing glasses, a black suit and tie and the other men are wearing suits. Serge greets them.

"Vladimir, I've met with my contact at the Russian Embassy and he has made official Russian Embassy cards for you, Ilva and Anton. He also has official Russian Embassy license plates for the new limousine. I'm having Desya install the license plates on the car which is downstairs in the garage. Those license plates will allow you to park in any no parking zone located in and around the FBI Headquarters".

Serge hands Vladimir a map and the cards. Vladimir gives Ilva and Anton each a card.

"Vladimir, I know how you must feel about the death of your brother, but if you see Mason or the girl, just follow them to where they are staying and don't do anything that might jeopardize our mission".

Vladimir stares at Serge and looks upset.

"Yes, Serge I understand".

"Good. Now take your men and go to the FBI headquarters and get yourselves accustomed to the place".

Vladimir is driving the limousine and Ilva and Anton are with him. He parks in a no parking zone across the street from the FBI headquarters. A traffic control officer comes over to the car. When he sees the official Russian Embassy license plates he waves and walks away. Vladimir and the men get out of the car, cross the street and enter the Federal Building. They go into an elevator with other people and Vladimir pushes a button for the seventeenth floor. The door closes and the elevator starts its upward journey, stopping at various floors to let people in and out. When it arrives at the seventeenth floor, the door opens and Vladimir and his men get out and looks around. An FBI agent comes out of an office.

"Do you have an appointment ?"

Vladimir and his men take out their Russian Embassy cards and show them to the FBI agent. Vladimir shakes his head.

"I'm sorry, I mistakenly thought we had an appointment today. Sorry".

The FBI agent looks at Vladimir's card. Then the agent takes out his own card and hands it to Vladimir.

"Please feel free to call me if you have any questions".

Vladimir smiles at the agent.

"I certainly will, sir. Thank you".

Vladimir and his men cross the street and get in the limousine.

"If any of you go back in there and anyone asks you for identification, show them your Russian Embassy badge. Mason and

Trishka could be staying up there, at the FBI headquarters".

Serge and Vladimir are sitting in the living room of Serge's house. Serge turns to Vladimir.

"I had my real estate broker check to see how many other houses the FBI owns. There are only three other places and they are all rented to FBI agents. Therefore, Mason and the woman are going to have to be accommodated in a safe house or some other place that the FBI feels comfortable with".

"I want them dead, Serge".

Serge stares at Vladimir.

"I know you do. But for now, we must find where they are hiding".

John, Trishka and Sam are in a small room in the FBI headquarters on the seventeenth floor of the Federal Building. Three small bunk beds and a desk comprise the room's furniture. Trishka looks at John.

"Every time I have to go to the bathroom, I have to get permission from the guard outside our door. I can't take much more of this John".

John shakes his head.

"I know Trish. I spoke to agent David Williams today and he said he's going to find us a safe place where we can live until they find Vladimir and the other Russian mafia men who are after us. I wish I could tell David what Vladimir looks like, but he must have changed his appearance so drastically that he can't be recognized. Just like Yuri did".

Trishka looks at John . . . hesitates.

"I hope you haven't told them about . . . .".

"Your head? No, I've told no one".

Trishka wraps her arms around John and weeps.

"I love you".

CHAPTER 18

John's cell phone rings. He clicks it on.

"Peter . . . what's going on?". Peter James the policeman is at his desk at the North Hollywood Police Station.

"John, I think we found the guy who killed your wife". John looks out the window in the room at the FBI building. He appears amazed.

"My God . . . how did you find the son of a bitch?"

Peter responds.

"We had a search warrant for the guy's house because he's been dealing cocaine. We found Sara's purse in a closet. Inside the purse was her driver's license and some of her credit cards".

John is now sitting down on one of the cots.

"What's the prick's name?"

Peter is looking through paper work on his desk.

"His name is Steve Crew and the District Attorney is going to have him as part of a line up. Can you bring your son in to see if he can identify the guy?"

The line up consists of eight men who are standing in the line up room in the District Attorney's office. They are suspects in a cocaine smuggling gang.

They are also there to see if Sam can identify the man who killed his mother. Sam, John and Peter are standing behind the one way window. Sam points to Steve Crew.

"He's the one who killed mom!"

Sam becomes hysterical and begins crying and sobbing. Another man in the room points to Steve Crew and one other in the line up as two of the cocaine smugglers. Peter then has the suspects taken out and goes into the hall. He speaks to the district attorney's assistant and comes back into the room where John and Sam are. Moments later, Steve Crew is brought into the room handcuffed. John grabs him by the throat and yells at him.

"You're dead motherfucker!"

John tries to smash Crew in the face, but he is stopped by Peter and the assistant district attorney. The door opens and District Attorney Michael Patterson comes in.

"Mister Crew, you are charged with murder and also the illegal sale of cocaine".

Two police officers come into the room. Patterson pushes Crew towards the officers.

"Take him to booking immediately".

The police officers take Crew out of the room. John holds Peter's hand.

"Thank you Peter . . . . thank you".

Sam, who is still crying hugs Peter.

"You found the man who took my mother from me".

"He's going to pay for what he did to her for the rest of his life. That's a promise, Sam".

One of Serge's fake DWP men comes into Serge's living room and hands Serge the tiny camera that Serge gave him. Serge looks at the picture on the camera's screen.

"When did you take this picture Desya?"

"Yesterday. It took me hours to get the picture clear enough to see".

"It's hard to tell whether the woman is Trishka Perova, but it looks like her, Desysa".

"We can't go back there Serge. The DWP inspector came today and told us to leave because the power was working now".

"You and Evgni did an excellent job. Now the truck must be repainted and all references on it to the DWP must be removed".

"Evgni and I will take care of that tomorrow, Serge". That evening Serge and Vladimir are sitting at the dining room table in Serge's house.

"We're in luck Vladimir. The FBI headquarters had an opening for a janitor and I had someone I know apply and it looks like he'll get the job".

"When would he start working?"

"Craig will start right after they do a background check on him".

"Do you think he'll pass the background check?"

Serge shakes his head "yes".

"Yes I do. A few years ago Craig worked in DC as a janitor for Senator Brighton. While he was there I helped take care of his sick father who was my neighbor. When his father had a heart attack, Craig came back to Los Angeles and stayed with him until he died. I know Craig will get a high recommendation because the senator liked his work and hated to see him leave DC. I told Craig I was looking for Mason and Trishka for personal reasons. I gave him pictures of them. Craig told me he owes me for watching his father and he said he'd let me know if he sees Mason or Trishka."

Vladimir clicks his wine glass against Serge's wine glass.

John, Trishka and Sam are eating dinner from a tray in their small living quarters at the FBI headquarters. Trishka puts her fork down.

"This food is terrible, John".

"I know, but we're not allowed out of here".

"Can't we just order some food to go from a restaurant and have someone pick it up for us?"

"I'll ask agent Williams tomorrow, Trish. He gets in about eight thirty in the morning".

Sam gives John a thumbs up.

"Thanks dad".

Trishka tries to turn on the television set, but it doesn't work. She looks over at John.

"The tv's broken".

John opens the door and looks at the guard.

"Do you think you can find us a tv set that works? We'd really appreciate it".

The guard gives John a tired look.

"I'll see if I can find one".

"Thanks".

Later John, Trishka and Sam are in their separate bunk beds asleep.

There's a loud knock at the door. John opens his eyes.

"Yes?"

"It's the guard. I found a tv set that works".

John gets out of bed and stumbles to the door in his pajamas. Trishka is in pajamas, sitting up in her bed. The guard walks in with a small tv set.

"Would you like me to hook it up?"

Trishka yawns.

"Yes, please".

The guard removes the wires from the broken tv and hooks up the one he brought in. He turns it on and it works but the screen is small and rather fuzzy. He carries the broken tv out and John shuts the door.

"I hate this place, John".

"I told you I'm going to talk to agent Williams tomorrow morning. I hate this place too". Sam stands up.

"So do I".

John climbs in Trishka's bunk bed, but it's much too small for both of them. He kisses her and starts to stroke her body but she looks over at Sam who's watching them. She pulls back. John looks upset as he gets into his bed.

Trishka gets up, comes over to John and puts her arms around him. Just as she begins kissing him, the guard starts talking loudly on his cell phone outside their door. Trishka raises her head and looks into John's eyes.

"I'm sorry John".

"It's ok, Trish".

She gets up, goes back to her bunk bed and turns off the light.

The next morning agent Williams is sitting behind his desk when John opens the door and walks in.

"Good morning David . . . hope you had a good night's sleep". "I'm sorry John. I know it must be hard for you and Trishka". "Have you had any luck finding a safe house where Trish and I can stay?"

"Not yet. You know, John your lives are in great danger outside of this building and until we find somewhere safe, you, Trishka and your son must stay here. President Farley has made that clear. There is one possibility however, that you and Trishka might want to consider".

John looks pleased.

CHAPTER 19

"During World War 2 our government constructed some underground safe houses that were to be used in case of an atomic attack"

"Yes, I've heard about them".

"There's a safe house about one hundred fifty five feet underground just a few miles from here, but it needs to be updated and cleaned".

John looks amazed.

"What's it like?"

"It has a kitchen, three bathrooms, a living room, two offices and two large bedrooms. I was going to wait until my crew was finished fixing it up before I mentioned it to you, but I think you, your son and Trishka would really like to stay there as a temporary place to live, and I think it would be much safer for you three there than it is up here. I was out there yesterday with my crew and we figured it would take about a week to make the place livable".

"Where is it?"

"There's a small abandoned parking lot right next to the VA Cemetery off Sepulveda Boulevard. The elevator to the safe house is covered by a flat steel door that's covered with asphalt, so it looks like just another parking place on the lot. The door is hinged and when it's opened you just walk down a few stairs to the elevator which takes you to the living quarters".

"Sounds good to me . . . I'll talk it over with Trish".

John, Trishka and Sam are sitting on John's bunk bed.

"The only thing that I don't like is that it's over one hundred fifty feet underground and there aren't any windows. But agent Williams thinks it is a really safe place for us to stay for now".

Trishka looks at John, puts her hand on his leg and smiles.

"Anything is better than this place, John".

"Ok, agent Williams will take us there in a few days to see how we like it". Trishka is really excited. She kisses John and dances around the room.

"I can hardly wait!" Sam looks at John.

"It sounds like a fun place, dad". Everybody laughs.

Serge is in his living room with Craig who is now a janitor at the FBI headquarters.

"Are you certain the man and woman you saw are John Mason and Trishka Perova?"

"Yes. A few days ago, a guard in front of room 1709 asked me if I would go to a restaurant in Westwood to get three lunches to go. I told him I would, then he gave me money and told me to tell the clerk at the restaurant that I was picking up food for some people at FBI headquarters because the FBI gets a discount there. I drove to the restaurant, got the lunches and went back to room 1709. I gave the guard the food, he knocked on the door and when it opened, I saw both Mason and Trishka. There was a young boy there too.

"You're positive they were Mason and Trishka?"

"Yes. They're the man and woman in the pictures you gave me. Why are you looking for them?"

"Because they promised to invest in my social club, but they never paid and because they lied, it cost me a shit load of money. I just want to talk to them about it. Thank you for finding them Craig and please don't say anything about me to them".

"Don't worry Serge, I won't . . . and I don't blame you for being upset They made a deal with you and reneged. That's happened to me before too, with someone I thought was my friend".

Serge is sitting behind his desk in his office above the Russian club when Vladimir comes in.

"They're living in room 1709 at the FBI headquarters, Vladimir".

"From our surveillance of the building we saw that there are only a few guards posted after midnight".

"Vladimir, I don't think it's wise to try and force our way into FBI headquarters".

"What if we dress like Mexican gang members?"

"Let me think about it Vladimir. You told me that all of your men are fluent in Spanish, so if you guys go in there speak only in Spanish so anyone who hears you will think you are from a Mexican gang".

"Serge . . . I must get my hands on Mason and Trishka for what they did to Yuri".

Serge starts to say something, but Vladimir turns around and stares at Serge.

"Nothing will stand in my way. They killed my brother!"

A few nights later Vladimir, Ilva and Anton are sitting in a parked car down the street from FBI headquarters. They are all wearing black pants, gloves and have black hoodies covering their heads. They get out of the car and walk down the street until they are across from the FBI headquarters. The area is deserted and quiet. They cross the street and walk up to the front door which is locked. There is a guard sitting behind a desk inside reading a newspaper. Vladimir and his men take out their pistols which have silencers. Vladimir points his pistol at the guard and shoots him in the head. Then he breaks the window which activates an alarm. Vladimir and the other men run to the elevator, go inside and push button 17. The elevator begins its ascent and stops at the seventeenth floor. The door opens and two guards are standing there with their guns pointed at the door. Vladimir and his men drop to the floor and immediately fire their pistols at the guards, killing one and wounding the other. The men run down to room 1709. The door is locked, so Vladimir kicks it open. They walk around the room, which is completely empty. Vladimir looks amazed. Then they rush down the hall to the emergency exit, open the door and run down the stairs When they reach the first floor they see police officers getting out of their cars across the street and coming towards the building, but before the police get to the building, Vladimir and his men are able to sneak out the rear through the emergency exit and run down the back of the building to an alley and then to their car without being seen.

Vladimir, Ilva and Anton walk into Serge's Russian club office about a half hour later. Serge is sitting behind his desk. They have taken off their hoodies and gloves and now look like regular patrons of the club. Vladimir looks bewildered.

"They've been taken to another location, Serge".

Serge puts his feet on the desk.

"It must have been after working hours or Craig would have seen them leave".

Vladimir hits his fist against the palm of his other hand.

"I hope they weren't taken out of Los Angeles".

Serge gives Vladimir a worried look.

"That's possible".

Vladimir hits his open hand with his fist again.

"Shit!"

Agent Williams is showing John, Trishka and Sam around the underground safe house in the morning.

"The police couldn't find any fingerprints or anything else that might have identified the men who broke into the FBI building and shot the guards, but the guard who was wounded heard the men speaking Spanish, which means that the men could have been from a Mexican gang. The really strange thing is that for some reason they broke into room 1709. I asked everyone who was on the

17th floor that day, and no one noticed anything suspicious going on with room 1709".

David, John, Trishka and Sam sit down at the dining room table.

"I don't want any of you leaving this safe house unless I give you permission in which case you will be accompanied by guards".

Williams turns on the flat screen tv on the wall above them. He changes channels until he comes to the latest news channel. A commercial is just ending, then the newscaster continues.

"As of this moment, nobody knows why the FBI headquarters was broken into which caused the deaths of two guards. However, there was a witness whose name and identity cannot be revealed who saw what looked like three gang members dressed in black, wearing head coverings leave the building through the back entrance. The police are investigating this as we speak".

Sam looks frightened and goes to the bathroom. Williams shuts off the tv and turns to John and Trishka.

"Can either of you think of any reason why Mexican gang members would be looking for you?"

John looks up at the ceiling, "It may have had something to do with my killing of Manuel Gomez a Mexican gang member who tried to kill President Farley, but how would Gomez' buddies know where to look for me?"

"They wouldn't. Perhaps the motive was just to rob the guards".

John paces around the room.

"But why would the go to room 1709?"

CHAPTER 20

An agitated President Farley is sitting in his chair behind his desk in the Oval Office and Vice President Ames is standing in the middle of the room.

"Roger, last night a terrorist was on a city bus in Austin, Texas carrying a suitcase with a small nuclear weapon inside. Luckily, the man sitting next to him was able to rip the suitcase from him before the guy had a chance to push the blue flashing button inside the suitcase. The son of a bitch is now locked down in Austin and refuses to say one word. If he would have been able to push that button, probably everyone on the bus plus people within a mile radius would be dead. Two days ago, the Russian police found a man carrying a suitcase on a train to Moscow which contained a nuclear device. He said it was a water filtration machine, but when the scientists took the device apart they discovered that it was a nuclear bomb. When the Russian authorities confronted the man, he tried to get away so they killed him. Therefore, Roger it is absolutely imperative that we find a way to re-activate our K Fifty Five computer".

"I've got sixteen men working around the clock trying to find a solution to the problem mister President. But so far, no luck".

President Farley remains silent for a short time, then begins to speak.

"What's going on with John Mason?"

"Well sir, Mason, his son and Trishka Perova were moved to an underground facility yesterday. Then, as I told you, what appeared to be gang members with hoodies covering their heads, broke into the FBI headquarters, killing two guards and wounding a third. They did break into room 1709 where Mason and Trishka were staying before they were moved to the safe house, but the guys also broke into other rooms on the seventeenth floor, so nothing they did seems to have anything to do with Mason or Trishka Perova . . . unless".

"Unless what Roger?"

"Unless it had something to do with Mason's killing of Manuel Gomez, one of the leaders of the Mexican mafia, when Mason was a Secret Agent here in DC".

"If Mason hadn't shot Gomez, Gomez would have thrown the hand grenade he was holding at me and I would've been killed".

"I know sir, and I also know that the Mexican mafia always tries to avenge the killing of their leaders".

President Farley stares at Ames.

"You know Rog . . . agent Rick Jubas, one of my best friends was killed by someone with his head covered like the men who broke into the FBI headquarters so his killing might be related in some way to that break in or what Mason did to Gomez. I want a thorough investigation done regarding the break in as well as a renewed review of the Jubas murder".

President Farley looks away then turns back to Ames.

"I know you'll keep me posted on all I'm asking for Roger . . . and I really appreciate what you're doing".

"Thank you sir".

It's morning in the underground safe house. Agent Williams, John, Trishka and Sam are sitting at the dining room table. Sam is eating cereal and the others are drinking coffee.

"John, Judge Warren wants Sam to testify at Steve Crew's murder trial which starts next Monday. I'll send him to the Criminal Courts Building with six FBI agents to make certain he's protected".

John looks around the room silently for a few moments.

"You're certain Sam will be safe?"

Agent Williams shakes his head "yes".

"Absolutely".

Trishka holds Sam who begins to cry.

"I want the man who killed my mom put in prison".

That night in Serge's home, Serge is sitting on the couch in the living room reading the newspaper. He hears the front door bell ring, goes to the door and opens it. Vladimir is standing there. Serge is holding the newspaper and points to an article on the front page.

"Mason's son is going to testify at his mother's murder trial Monday".

Vladimir is totally surprised.

"Where is the trial going to be held?"

"Downtown at the Criminal Courts Building where I was questioned about buying the Russian club".

Vladimir stares at Serge.

"Send someone to the courtroom. I want Mason's son followed after the judge finishes for the day".

It's morning in Los Angeles Criminal Courtroom Number 109. Sam is sitting in the witness chair. Six FBI agents are sitting next to each other on a bench with other people watching the proceedings in the spectator section. One of the people in the spectator section is Anton, sent there by Serge. The jurors are watching and listening as the District Attorney questions Sam. Steve Crew is sitting at a table with his attorney. Crew is handcuffed and is wearing an orange jump suit. The District Attorney speaks.

"Now, son. Tell us in your own words what happened that day to your mother".

Sam points to Steve Crew.

"I was hiding under my bed watching that man holding a gun against my mother's head. He started laughing and my mother started screaming. Then he shot her in the head two times . . . and blood . . .".

Sam stops speaking and begins to hysterically cry.

"Samuel, would you like to take a break for awhile?"

Sam looks at the District Attorney and shakes his head "no".

"Blood went flying out of my mother's head and that man kept laughing. When my mother fell to the floor, he kicked her in the head, took her purse and left the room".

"So he never saw where you were hiding?".

"No sir".

John and Trishka are watching the trial on television in the safe house. Trishka is crying and John is holding her.

Judge Warren speaks.

"Does the defense have anything further?"

The defense attorney stands up.

"Yes your honor, just one more question". The judge looks over at Sam and the defense attorney begins to speak.

"Now Samuel, you told us you saw my client holding a pistol to your mother's head and shoot her, yet he didn't see or look for you, is that correct?"

"Yes sir. I was hiding way under the bed looking up and he never looked down, not once".

"And you didn't make a sound? Don't you think that was unusual Samuel that you didn't cry out?" Sam shakes his head.

About one hour later John, Trishka and agent Williams are still watching the trial on television as Judge Warren speaks.

"I am advised that the jury has reached a verdict".

The presiding juror hands the verdict sheet to the bailiff who delivers it to judge Warren. Judge Warren reads the sheet and hands it back to the bailiff who gives it to the presiding juror to read out loud.

"We the jury find Steve Crew guilty of first degree murder with special circumstances in the killing of Sara Mason".

The defense attorney stands up.

"Your honor, the defense requests a bail hearing".

The judge answers.

"There shall be no bail hearing in this case. The defendant is remanded to custody immediately".

Two police officers escort Crew out of the courtroom in handcuffs.

The judge turns to the jury, "The jurors are excused and I thank you all for your services".

Everyone in the courtroom stands as the jurors walk out and the judge leaves the bench. The people in the spectator section start leaving the courtroom.

Sam goes over to the six FBI agents who walk him out. Anton waits for a few other people to leave behind the agents and Sam, then follows them out of the courtroom. The agents and Sam walk down the hall then go into a room that has the word "private" in large letters above it. Anton goes to the door after it closes and finds that it is locked. He takes out his cell phone and clicks it on.

Serge and Vladimir are in Serge's living room watching the proceedings on television. Serge's cell phone rings and he opens it.

"Serge, it's Anton. They took the boy into a private locked room down the hall from the courtroom".

Serge answers. "When I was questioned by the DA about my purchase of the Russian club, it was done in the private office down the hall from the same courtroom. That office has an elevator that leads to a restricted parking garage with a private exit. I want you to go around the back of the building in your car and wait by that private exit. It has the word "private" in large red letters on the wall. That's where they will be driving out with Mason's son. Do it immediately Anton, so you'll be able to follow their car to wherever they take the boy".

A few minutes later the FBI agents and Sam are in a large black SUV which is coming out of the private exit. Anton is across the street in his car. He sees Sam sitting in the back seat. He follows the SUV to the abandoned parking lot in West Los Angeles where it stops. Anton continues driving down the street then stops, gets out of his car and walks back toward the abandoned parking lot. Anton sits on a wall next to a house and watches as one of the FBI agents gets out of the SUV and unlocks the gate, then gets back in the vehicle and it is driven across the lot and stops next to what appears to be a parking space covered with asphalt. Three agents get out, then Sam gets out. The other three agents stay in the SUV and drive back to the street. The vehicle stops for a moment while one of the agents gets out, winds the chain around the fence and locks it. Then he gets back in the SUV with the other two agents and they drive off. One of the three agents left behind in the parking lot with Sam, bends down to rows of large pebbles right next to the parking space. He presses the pebbles in a certain order. There is a loud clicking sound. Then an underground motor slowly opens a large very thick steel door which, on the surface, looks like an asphalt parking space, but in reality opens to the entrance to the underground safe house. The three agents and Sam go inside and the steel door slowly closes. Unnoticed by the FBI agents, Anton is still sitting on the wall down the street, videotaping the entire process with a miniature camera. The three agents and Sam enter the living room of the safe house. John and Trishka rush over to Sam and hug him. Sam is sobbing. Trishka is holding him.

"I miss my mom so much".

Sam looks into Trishka's eyes.

"You are like a mother to me".

Tears run down Trishka's cheeks as she and Sam continue holding each other. John goes over and hugs both of them.

CHAPTER 21

Serge, Vladimir and Anton are standing in Serge's home office that afternoon. Serge looks at Anton.

"So the boy was taken to an empty fenced in parking lot and then a large steel door opened and they took him underground?"

"Yes Serge. The place was well disguised. The steel door concealing the entrance to the underground quarters must be at least five feet thick and very wide and heavy. I videotaped the whole thing".

Anton takes out his video taping device and plays the process for Serge and Vladimir to see. Then Anton pushes a button on the video machine for a close up look at the man who was bending down and touching the pebbles. Serge turns to Vladimir.

"It looks like that man was punching in a secret code. Play it again Anton".

Anton repeats the video clip of the man touching the pebbles, but it is impossible to know which pebbles he is touching because his other arm was blocking the view. Serge clicks his cell phone on.

"We've got to get that code".

Craig is sweeping the floor in the hall at the FBI building. His cell phone rings and he clicks it on.

"Hello Serge. No . . . . I don't know where the FBI took Mason and the woman. Nobody told me".

Craig listens to Serge for a short time then shakes his head and frowns.

"Your telling me that you know where they are Serge? You had the boy followed? That doesn't seem right".

The line on Craig's phone clicks, someone is calling Craig.

"I'll have to get back to you Serge".

"Yes sir, agent Williams I'll be right there".

Craig shuts down his cell phone and frowns again. Craig walks into FBI agent Williams office with a worried look on his face. Williams is sitting behind his desk.

"Sit down Craig".

Craig sits down in a chair facing agent Williams.

"You know that Senator Brighton is a good friend of mine and speaks very highly of you. He told me that you were exposed to government secrets when he forgot to hide the top secret documents he mistakenly left on his office desk. He said that you saw the papers which contained red underlined sentences and you told him that you would never tell a living soul what the documents revealed when you gave the papers back to Brighton. That's why I hired you".

Craig's expression changes to one of relief.

"Yes sir".

Agent Williams appears very serious.

"Now, Craig I'm going to tell you something very, very confidential and you must never let anyone know what I'm about to disclose to you. Do you understand?"

"I promise sir, I'll never mention it to anyone".

"Ok . . . John Mason, his son Sam and Trishka Perova have been moved out of room 1709 to an underground facility not far from here. Your job is going to be keeping that place clean for them, bringing them food and supplies and you are to call me if you see anything suspicious. I mean anything! Is that clear Craig?"

Craig shakes his head "yes".

"Now here is the most important part of my disclosure to you. It is the code that will allow you to open the trap door and let you into the underground facility. This code must remain a secret because if the wrong individuals become aware of it, the people we are protecting would all be in great danger. I want you to promise me that you will never disclose the code I'm about to give you to anyone. Only myself and a very few of my most trusted agents know the code".

Craig holds out his hand and agent Williams shakes it.

"I promise you sir, on my life, I will never give the code to anyone".

"I believe you and trust you Craig. Thank you. Now I want you to memorize the code".

Williams shows Craig a picture of the fenced in parking lot.

"This abandoned parking lot is on Lookout Drive, the first street north of the VA Cemetery on Sepulveda Boulevard. Are you familiar with that area?"

"Yes sir I am. My oldest and dearest friend who was killed in Vietnam is buried there".

Williams shows Craig another picture of small stones next to what looks like a parking space but is the steel entrance door covered in asphalt.

"These stones are permanently locked in place next to the entrance to the underground facility. You'll notice that some of the stones look like numbers. Well, when the proper stones are pushed in a certain order, the locks holding the steel door unlock themselves and the door is opened by an underground motor. What you must do to open the door is touch the rocks in this order, and this order only. Repeat after me. The first number is 2".

Craig repeats "2".

"7".

Craig repeats "7".

"9".

Craig repeats "9".

"4".

Craig repeats "4".

"8".

Craig repeats "8".

"And the last number, Craig is 3".

Craig repeats "3".

"Now, Craig repeat the code".

Craig repeats the numbers from memory.

"2, 7, 9, 4, 8, 3".

"Now, Craig I want you to write those numbers down in the order I gave them to you".

Craig writes them on a piece of paper.

"Good, now you're to go to the parking lot and open the steel door. I'm calling the three agents who are there to let them know you are coming".

Agent Williams hands Craig a small key.

"This key is for the lock that holds the chain together and when you unlock that lock and unwind the chain, you'll be able to open the barbed wire fence door which will let you into the parking lot. Okay, Craig, repeat the code".

Craig stares at Williams

"2, 7, 9, 4, 8,3".

"Excellent. Now get into your car, drive out there, open the steel door and take the elevator down to the safe house".

"Thank you sir and I promise, I won't betray your secret".

Craig, the three FBI agents, John Trishka and Sam are all standing in the kitchen of the underground safe house. Craig speaks.

"I'll come on Monday, Wednesday and Friday at exactly ten in the morning to clean the place. Please call agent Williams before I come with any requests you may have for food or anything else and I'll bring it with me".

John shakes Craig's hand.

"Thank you Craig".

Serge and Vladimir are sitting on a couch in Serge's living room when there is a knock on the front door. Serge looks at Vladimir, goes to the door and opens it. Craig walks in.

"You wanted to see me?"

Serge stares at Craig.

"What were you doing at that abandoned parking lot next to the VA Cemetery today?"

Craig seems puzzled.

"That's my business".

Serge raises his voice.

"Tell us what you were doing there!"

"You were spying on me?"

"One of my men saw you there".

Craig gives Serge a nasty look. Vladimir steps in front of Serge and yells at Craig.

"Tell us what you were doing there and how you got the iron door to open!"

Craig looks down at the floor.

"I can't".

Vladimir grabs Craig by the neck.

"You will tell us! Your wife's name is Natalie and your daughter's name is Veronica and we know where you live. If you want them to remain alive you tell us what we want to know. Otherwise . . . ."

Vladimir squeezes Craig's neck. Then lets go. Serge gets in Craig's face.

"We don't want to hurt you or your family, Craig. But we must find John Mason and Trishka Perova. I hope you think your family is more important to you than Mason and Perova".

Vladimir slaps Craig in the face, then grabs him by the hair.

"You've got thirty seconds to tell us".

Craig looks at Vladimir in total fear. His body is shaking.

"Gi . . . give me a piece of paper and a pencil".

Serge gives Craig a piece of paper and pencil from his desk. Craig writes something on the paper and hands it to Serge. Serge looks at what Craig wrote then says.

"2,7,9,4,8,3 . . . that's the secret code?"

Craig answers in a fearful whisper.

"There are rocks next to the parking spot which is really an iron cover under which there is a safe house where the people you want are living. Those rocks are shaped like numbers. You push each numbered rock in the order I wrote down and the iron cover will unlock and allow you to enter the safe house. Now promise me you won't hurt my family".

Vladimir spits on Craig. Then he takes out his knife, opens it and runs his finger over the blade. Craig tries to get away, but Serge grabs him.

Vladimir pulls Craig's head back and slits his throat.

John, Trishka and Sam are in the living room of the underground safe house with the three FBI agents. One agent hands John a Glock 23 and a handful of extra cartridges. John checks the gun to make certain it's loaded, then puts it and the extra cartridges in a bookcase above the couch he's standing in front of. Sam excitedly watches what John is doing. One of the agents turns to John.

"Don't respond to anyone who may come here unless agent Williams has called you first".

The three FBI agents get in the safe house elevator and get out when it stops. One of the agents pushes a large red button on the wall and the steel door opens.

The agents walk up the stairs then out onto the parking lot. One of the agents gets on his knees and touches the secret code to the rocks next to the steel door. The door closes and the agents walk to the fence surrounding the parking lot. One of the agents opens the lock holding the chain and they step onto the sidewalk. The agent then wraps the chain around the fence and locks it. The black SUV is waiting for them at the curb. The three agents get in the SUV and it drives away.

Later, a van pulls up at the curb across from the abandoned parking lot. Vladimir, Serge and the rest of the men who drove in from Palm Springs get out of the van. Vladimir cuts the chain on the fence and they all walk into the parking lot.

John, Trishka and Sam are at the dining room table having dinner. All of a sudden they hear a noise above them. John goes to the bookcase and retrieves his pistol. John whispers to Trishka.

"Go to our bedroom with Sam and both of you get under the bed".

Trishka stands there and whispers.

"I want to help you John".

John points to the door.

"Go!"

Trishka takes a large kitchen knife in one hand and takes Sam by the other hand and goes out the kitchen door. She and Sam go to the bedroom and slide under the bed. John is on his cell phone,

"You haven't sent anyone else here? Someone's just opened the secret door!"

John clicks his cell phone off, pulls the couch away from the wall and gets behind it. Moments later, Serge, Vladimir and the rest of the Russian men walk silently by the kitchen and look in. There's no one in the kitchen, so they continue down the hall to the dining room. They can be heard whispering as they walk into the dining room where they see dishes of food on the table. They are all carrying the pistols that Serge gave them when they came in from Palm Springs. John moves silently behind the couch until his head sticks out from the side of the couch. Just as Anton turns and looks toward the couch, John's hand comes out holding the pistol. Anton yells.

"It's Mason!"

John shoots Anton in the head as the rest of the men drop to the floor and begin shooting toward the couch that John is now behind. Three of the Russian men crawl toward the couch. Suddenly, John's head can be seen again and his hand comes out with the gun. He shoots all three men, killing them, then instantly slides back behind the couch before the other men have time to raise their guns and shoot him.

There is no movement from John. Serge, Vladimir and the remaining two Russian men pull the dining room table over on its side which protects them from any shots that John might fire in their direction. They are all facing away from the dining room door when Trishka appears in the doorway holding the knife. She runs into the room screaming and stabs one of the men in the neck with the knife. John comes out from behind the couch and starts shooting at the dining room table which is upended. Vladimir turns and points his gun at Trishka, pulls the trigger and a bullet hits her in the shoulder. John runs around the table with his pistol blasting. He shoots Serge in the forehead, then shoots the other man in the side of the head, leaving Vladimir as the last Russian bad man alive. Trishka is lying on the floor bleeding from her shoulder wound. John points his gun at Vladimir and pulls the trigger, but his gun is out of ammunition. Vladimir calmly points his pistol at John and yells.

"Now you will pay for killing my brother!"

Vladimir points his pistol at John's head, but doesn't see Sam coming up behind him. Sam gives Vladimir a side kick to the head which knocks Vladimir to the floor and the pistol falls from his hand. John grabs the pistol and points it at Vladimir's head.

"Die . . . you son of a bitch!"

John pulls the trigger and the bullet blows Vladimir's head apart.

The next morning, John, Trishka with a bandaged shoulder and Sam are sitting on the couch in agent William's office. Williams is sitting in his chair behind his desk. Williams faces John.

"President Farley wants to speak to you tomorrow in person at nine in the morning".

Trishka gets up from the couch.

"I have something important to discuss with the President. Is it ok if I come with John?"

Agent Williams looks over at John, then turns to Trishka.

"I'll ask the President".

Later that evening, John and Trishka are in Sam's room at John's house in Sherman Oaks.

Sam is under the covers in his bed. Trishka goes over and hugs him and so does John. John looks at Trishka.

"We made it through hell and back Trish".

John strokes Sam's head.

"Goodnight my son".

Trishka kisses Sam's forehead.

"Goodnight Sam".

"Night mom and dad".

John and Trishka smile at each other after hearing what Sam said and then John kisses Trishka. They get up and leave Sam's room, closing the door behind them.

Later, in the master bedroom, John is in bed watching the large screen television. Trishka comes out of the bathroom in her bra and panties and moves toward the bed in a slow sexy motion. She sits on the bed and John changes her shoulder bandage.

"How's the shoulder?"

Trishka runs her fingers down John's chest.

"I'll live."

She gets under the covers and John turns off the television with his remote. Then he reaches for Trishka who gives him a long sexy kiss. He starts to get on top of her but she pulls back.

"Oh Trish . . . I'm so sorry. It's your head and now it's your shoulder".

Trishka smiles and nods.

"John, I want to discuss what Ivan did to me with President Farley tomorrow".

"I thought you didn't want anyone to know what they did to you".

"There may be a safe way to remove the chip the doctor put in my head and if so, the K Fifty Five computer in DC might come back to life. I really don't know what restoring the K Fifty Five would mean, but I would like to discuss it with the President".

"Well I'm sure President Farley would want to talk to you about it, so come with me tomorrow morning to agent Williams office.

Trishka strokes John's chest then climbs on top of him. She kisses his lips, shoulders, then his chest and he kisses her breasts. Then he turns the light off and they both begin moaning.

At seven thirty in the morning John's cell phone rings, waking John and Trishka up. John picks up the phone.

"Hello, oh yes David, we're up. He wants us at the White House today? Ok, we'll be at LAX at eight thirty".

Trishka sits up. She's naked from the waist up.

"What's happening John?"

"President Farley wants you and me to come to the White House today".

Trishka looks excited.

"We have to be on the private jet that's reserved for us by eight thirty so let's get ready".

CHAPTER 22

John, Trishka and Sam are taking off from a runway at LAX in a Gulfstream G550 jet. A sexy looking flight attendant bends over showing John her cleavage while she refills his coffee cup. The attendant walks away and Trishka pokes John in the side then they both laugh. John, Trishka and Sam get out of the jet in DC and are escorted to a limousine. After driving for awhile, the driver turns into a street that leads to the White House. The limo stops at a guard gate and after the driver discusses something with the guard and points to his passengers, he is allowed to take the limo right up to the front steps of the White House and everyone gets out.

President Farley's secretary, Susan Polk stands as John, Trishka and Sam come into the outer office. Susan smiles.

"President Farley is waiting for you".

Susan opens Farley's door. President Farley is sitting in his leather chair behind his massive desk. Vice President Ames is standing. John,

Trishka and Sam are escorted into the Oval Office by Susan and President Farley gets up.

"Good afternoon folks. Have a seat on the couch".

They walk to the couch and sit down. President Farley comes over to them. They all get up and shake his hand. Farley turns and looks at Sam.

"First, I want to say how much I want to thank you Sam for what you did that saved your father's life yesterday. You know, he saved my life too".

Sam stands up and looks very excited and happy.

"Yes, mister President I know about the hand grenade incident. I just want you to know that you have my total respect".

Sam sits down on the couch. John stands up.

"President Farley, I believe Trishka has something that's extremely important to discuss with you and I'm wondering if you would like to be alone with her while she talks to you about it".

Farley looks at Trishka.

"What would you like to do Miss Perova?"

"I . . . I would very much like to discuss an urgent matter with you privately sir".

Farley pushes a button on his office phone.

"Segram, come in please".

A large uniformed guard opens the door and walks in.

"Please take John and Sam to the cafeteria".

"Yes mister President".

John and Sam follow Segram out of the Oval Office and President Farley walks over to the couch.

A few minutes later, Trishka and President Farley are sitting next to each other on the couch. Farley is looking at the back of Trishka's head.

"So my boss in Russia Ivan Sakalov had a microchip from the brain of the Russian K Fifty Five computer injected into the back of my skull and he told me that the chip contained all the information needed to make another K Fifty Five computer and the information in the chip would allow your K Fifty Five computer in the United States to continue running".

Farley looks at the back of Trishka's head. She gently puts her finger on the dot under her hair on the back of her skull.

"This is where it went in".

"Why have you kept it a secret?"

"Because Ivan said that if anyone tried to take the chip out that I would die".

Farley stares at her.

"A friend of mine is probably the best doctor there is when it comes to anything to do with the brain or nervous system. He works at Johns Hopkins hospital and if you give me your permission, I would like him to discuss the matter with you".

Trishka looks afraid and she remains silent for a few moments.

"I give you my permission, mister President".

President Farley, John and Trishka are sitting down in separate chairs in doctor Frank Mellew's office. Mellew is sitting in his chair behind his desk. Doctor Mellew looks at Trishka.

"I cannot promise you that the procedure I would use to remove the microchip is one hundred percent safe, but the x-rays show that the chip is encased in a tiny lead ball. The x-rays also show that the lead ball has not been damaged. I'm thinking of trying a totally new procedure to remove the material from your skull . . . a procedure that has never been tried before, but one that I think is many times safer than any other procedure now in existence. Now Miss Perova, it is completely up to you whether or not you will allow me to try and remove the materials".

"I'm really afraid, doctor Mellew, but after what President Farley told me what miracles could be accomplished if the chip was removed from my skull safely, I am willing to let you try and remove it".

Trishka looks over at John with tears in her eyes. John comes over to her and holds her face in his hands. She looks up at him.

"Where is Sam?"

"He's at the White House. Thelma Farley, the president's wife is looking after him".

CHAPTER 23

Later, in the operating room Trishka is lying under a sheet on the operating table. John is standing next to her. Doctor Mellew is on the other side of the table. John reaches for Trishka's face, but doctor Mellew puts his hands up.

"It's ok if you touch her mister Mason, but first please put on these rubber gloves".

The doctor gives John a pair of rubber gloves. He puts them on and then touches Trishka's face.

"I love you Trish".

Trishka looks up at John with tears in her eyes.

"I love you too. Please tell Sam that I love him with all my heart".

Later in the operating room there are a number of men and women in hospital gowns standing around watching what doctor Mellew is preparing to do. Trishka is lying on her stomach on the table with plastic tubes inside her nose and a large plastic shell around her mouth.There is an anesthetic flowing into her arm from a plastic bag above the table. She is totally unconscious. Her head is held on both sides by two metal devices. Doctor Mellew has just finished shaving the area around the small dark protrusion in the back of her skull. Anthony Vickers, his assistant brings over a large round machine on wheels with a green flashing tube sticking out of its side. Assistant Vickers hands the flashing tube to doctor Mellew who places the large end of the tube around the protrusion in the back of Trishka's skull.

Mellew looks over at Vickers.

"Ok Tony, turn it up to twenty five hundred rpms".

"Yes, doctor".

Vickers turns a dial on the machine and the green flashing becomes extremely bright and the round end of the tube begins to spin. Doctor Mellew gently pushes on the tube which starts to go into Trishka's skull, then he stops pushing and puts up his hand very fast. In a loud voice he says to Vickers.

"Quickly Tony . . . turn it down to fifteen hundred rpms!"

Vickers turns the dial he has his hand on backwards and the green flashing gets dimmer. Doctor Mellew looks excited.

"I think it's working Tony!"

A few seconds later a small dark round object appears inside the green flashing plastic tube.

"Ok Tony, tum it back to zero rpms".

Vickers turns the dial back and doctor Mellew slowly pulls the end of the tube out of Trishka's skull. A small amount of blood comes out of the hole in her skull where the round object used to be.

"We've done it Tony!"

All the people in the room applaud doctor Mellew and he bows.

President Farley, Vice President Ames and the computer genius Sidney Manning are standing around Farley's desk in the Oval Office. On the desk is a small glass case which contains the tiny round lead device that was in Trishka's skull. Manning takes a small metal tool from his briefcase.

"This will tell us if what's inside that lead covering is of any value".

Manning reaches into his briefcase and removes what looks like a large pair of fingernail clippers.

"These clippers will cut through the lead covering without harming what's inside. Should I proceed mister President?"

Farley shakes his head "yes".

"Go ahead, Manning".

Manning gently places one end of the clippers onto a round piece of the lead covering and presses the two ends of the clippers together. Suddenly from inside the lead covering a shimmering, flashing red light can be seen. The tool that Manning previously removed from his briefcase gives off a blaring signal. Manning looks totally excited and yells.

"We've hit pay dirt mister President! I'll take this to Langley and put it inside our K Fifty Five".

President Farley appears overwhelmed.

"Call me the second you get there Sid!"

Later, President Farley is sitting behind his desk reading the newspaper. His secretary Susan runs in holding a cell phone.

"It's President Chernov. He says it's an emergency sir!"

Farley grabs the cell phone from Susan and yells into it.

"What's wrong President Chernov?"

President Chernov is in his office in the Kremlin on his cell phone.

"My undercover adviser just called me seconds ago and told me that the Kremlin is surrounded by vehicles containing atomic bombs set to go off in two minutes. I cannot get out of the building in that short time and since I only have a few more minutes to live, I want to tell you that you are my best friend and want to thank you for all that you have done for me".

CHAPTER 24

President Farley is standing behind his desk, stunned by what President Chernov has just told him. He starts to answer Chernov, but Vice President Ames interrupts him.

"It's Sidney Manning and it's an emergency, mister President!"

President Farley yells into his cell phone.

"Don't hang up President Chernov, I'll be right back!"

Farley takes Ames cell phone and in a frenzied voice says.

"What is it Manning?" Manning is on his cell phone in the computer room at Langley Air Force Base. He yells into the phone.

"Mister President, I put the microchip from Trishka Perova's head into our K Fifty Five computer and it's now working!"

President Farley yells into his cell phone.

"Manning I want you to immediately deactivate all nuclear devices in the vicinity of the Kremlin and the Russian Embassy . . . . Launch the deactivator right now!!"

Manning puts down his cell phone in the computer room at Langley, goes to the K Fifty Five computer keyboard and begins typing. The word "LAUNCHED" appears on the computer screen. Manning gets back on his cell phone.

"I launched the deactivator mister President and it's one hundred percent effective!"

President Farley puts down Ames' cell phone, picks his cell phone up and begins talking to President Chernov.

"The head of my computer facility has just deactivated all the nuclear devices in and around the Kremlin and the Russian Embassy".

There are ten uniformed soldiers in Chernov's office. Chernov says to the soldiers loud and clear in Russian.

"Get down to the street and stop all vehicles, then check them for anything that looks suspicious and arrest all persons in and around those vehicles".

Later in the official Russian Embassy garage, large suitcases are all open and piled up in the middle of the floor. President Chernov and Afanasei Gavrill, an expert in nuclear devices are standing next to the open suitcases. Gavrill turns to President Chernov and says in Russian.

"Mister President, by my estimation, there was enough nuclear material in those suitcases to level the Kremlin as well as everything within a twenty mile radius. I don't know how it was done, but in all my years as head of the Russian Nuclear Bureau, I've never seen anything like the deactivation of the nuclear material in those suitcases into useless rubble. It all seems like an impossibility, yet somehow the material was all reduced to garbage. In my opinion sir, it was a miracle. I'll have my men remove all the material from the garage and make certain all of it is totally deactivated".

"Thank you Gavrill".

"Your welcome mister President. But who do you think could possibly be responsible for this horrible event that could have occurred?"

"I don't know, perhaps the Chechen militants, but I'm going to get to the bottom of it and punish those responsible".

President Farley is sitting in his chair in the Oval Office talking to President Chernov on the telephone.

"I'm going to have another K Fifty Five computer made for you President Chernov. It will take awhile, but I feel the world will be much safer if we could stop the terrorists from being able to use atomic weapons against us. In the meantime, please send me a list of the countries you know will use nuclear energy only for peaceful purposes and I will not disturb them. Also, send me a list of countries and individual groups whom you think might use nuclear energy like the one that tried to use it on you today and I will freeze their capabilities." President Chernov answers.

"Yes, I most certainly will do that. I don't know how to thank you and your people for what you did today. You saved my life as well as the lives of thousands of my people. God bless you President Farley".

CHAPTER 25

Wedding arrangements, flowers, food, drinks, tables, chairs and a small beautiful portable wedding chapel are in a magical looking outdoor setting with a barn and horses in the background at the Bakersfield horse ranch. Many people are sitting in chairs in the designated area including President Farley, Vice President Ames, Russian President Chernov, FBI Agent David Williams, Sidney Manning, police officer Peter James, Lena Cheka's aunt, General Starker, Judge Warren who tried the Crew murder case, and many others. The entire area is surrounded by a contingent of Federal Marshals sent to guard both presidents and as well as all the other government individuals.

John and Trishka are in the master bedroom of the ranch house. John's wearing a black suit, white shirt and a bow tie. Trishka is wearing a white wedding dress.

"I know we're not supposed to be with each other at this time Trish, but I just wanted to see you before we're married. You are so beautiful".

"I love you so much John".

"I love you too Trish and so does my best man, Sam". They both laugh.

"Incidentally, the American-Russian Social Club is going to be a language school where English will be taught to foreign students".

"That's wonderful, John".

"My down payment and the proceeds from Rick and Marilyn's insurance policy has paid the entire purchase price for this horse ranch. Rick and Marilyn have no children or heirs. I put your name on the deed with mine and Sam's so now the three of us own this ranch free and clear."

Trishka rushes over to John and gives him a bear hug.

"Thank you for everything John. You are my lord and master". John smiles and kisses Trishka on the lips.

A short time later outside in the wedding area President Farley and Russian President Chernov are at the speaker's stand. President Farley is standing in front of the microphone.

"I'd like to say a few words at this joyous occasion. I am so very happy that John Mason and Trishka Perova are going to be man and wife. I want all of you to know that John there, saved my life a few years ago and he is my hero".

Farley moves away from the microphone and President Chernov moves to the front of the microphone.

"As you all know, I am the president of the Soviet Union and I am here today to congratulate John Mason and his beautiful wife to be, Trishka Perova. I want you to know that the other day, President Farley not only saved my life, but the lives of countless other people in my country by disarming over twenty atomic weapons, and for that I will be eternally grateful".

The orchestra begins playing "Here Comes The Bride" as John, Trishka and Sam walk slowly up the aisle to the portable wedding chapel where Judge Warren is waiting. They stop in front of the judge.

"Under the laws of the State of California, I now pronounce you man and wife".

Judge Warren looks at John and smiles.

"You may now kiss the bride".

John gives Trishka a strong hug and a long sexy kiss. The onlookers in the audience clap and shout "YES". As the audience continues clapping, John takes Trishka's hand and Trishka takes Sam's hand. They look at each other and smile as they slowly walk toward the barn and riding arena. As they walk through the open barn with horse stalls on either side, horses stick their heads out and whinny.

THE END